A Pardonable Offence

ANDREW LAFLECHE

A Pardonable Offence
Copyright © 2017 Andrew Lafleche

Published by Pub House Books
www.PubHouseBooks.com

Cover design by Richard Halawig

ISBN: 0-9947901-1-2
ISBN-13: 978-0-9947901-1-8

First Edition: June 2017

10 9 8 7 6 5 4 3 2 1

FOR KALI

CONTENTS

"SOMETIMES YOU HAVE TO
CROSS THE LINE JUST TO
REMEMBER WHERE IT LAYS."

-Anonymous, Somewhere

CLAYTON'S CABIN

No amount of wishing makes things so. Regardless, Clayton Jeffries wished. He wished the snow would stop. He wished this every day for as long as he'd been forgotten in this cabin wherever he was first forgotten from.

Outside the window the snow fell like it always fell. Clayton sat in his chair, face pressed against the glass, and counted the Shrubs. Why there were Shrubs this far north Clayton didn't know. He didn't wonder. He'd stopped wondering things months before. Now, Clayton just counted. Counting was less taxing than wondering. Eleven Shrubs he counted. Eleven Shrubs wrapped in burlap sheets. Eleven Shrubs frozen in the ground, wrapped in burlap sheets, covered in snow since he'd arrived.

If even they were Shrubs.

Sometimes, instead of thinking about why the Shrubs lived this far north, Clayton peered through the snowflakes and imagined the Shrubs were people wrapped in burlap sacks. The twine securing the burlap around the Shrubs he imagined as belts. Frozen Friar-looking people how he thought Friars would have looked if he'd been alive when Friars knocked door-to-door collecting money for the church, money for the poor. Always collecting for whatever Friars were always collecting for. Friars wearing their tattered burlap sacks as clothing.

Outside Clayton's window he imagined a clan of frozen Friars.

Forgotten Friars.

Forgotten Clayton.

Not really. No matter how lonely Clayton came to feel, he knew he wasn't *actually* forgotten. He knew *they'd* come for him; eventually. They wouldn't just leave him there. They couldn't;

the people conducting the experiment. The people he volunteered himself to. He knew this like someone who's dreaming knows they're dreaming but still can't wake up. This type of knowing didn't give him any comfort.

Sometimes through the snowflakes Clayton thought he saw the Friar-looking Shrubs standing in a row. Some days he saw them dressed in single file. Other days when Clayton caught a glimpse of the Shrubs through the sheet of white, he was certain he saw them huddled in a circle. In the center of the circle he imagined a barrel burning to keep the Shrubs warm.

In the beginning, when Clayton first arrived at the cabin, he thought maybe the snow stopped during the night, like how down south where he'd come from, how it only rained while everyone slept. After several months being cooped up in this one room cabin, after several months of stale air and relentless snowing, Clayton started staying awake through the night hoping to catch a glimpse of bare sky.

Hoping to see something other than white.

Hoping to see the Shrub people come to life.

Wishing for reprieve from whatever *this* was that he was experiencing.

Clayton Jefferies, all alone in this cabin, hoped and wished for things that would never be.

There never was bare sky. Only snow.

There never were sights to see. Only white.

The Shrubs wrapped in burlap sacks never came to life.

His wish for reprieve was never answered, most likely because for wishes to come true there needs to be a star to wish upon.

There never were any stars.

The red light on the camera dome blinked from the ceiling. Blink. Blink. Blink. Always blinking; night and day. Always snowing; day and night. Never knowing where the camera was pointed. Never knowing if even there was a camera inside the dome. Sometimes Clayton thought the dome was just a dome with a blinking light to make him think *they* were watching. The same type of fraud found in convenience stores, how the camera behind the clerk was most often a prop to deter would-be criminals from robbing the store.

Clayton thought about what this camera might be meant to deter him from.

He didn't dare speak to himself out loud. If *they* could hear, Clayton didn't want to appear crazy. Clayton wasn't crazy, at least that's what he assured himself, but he knew how an appearance often became an identity and that even the appearance of crazy might cause him to be locked away.

How Clayton found himself in this position, he wasn't quite certain. Surely there was an ad. It's fact he was recently laid off. They said he would be compensated for his time. As most things go in life, way often leads onto way. Six months of solitude. A single room cabin, somewhere up north. It would be good for him to get away. Everything would be provided. Stocked and locked.

"Stocked and locked," Clayton said out loud, immediately regretting his slip.

He pretended he didn't say it, as he wasn't sure whether the camera could hear him, and continued to stare out the window. Through the blowing snow Clayton thought he saw the Shrub people huddled in groups of three. He assured himself he must be seeing things. He knew there were only eleven Shrubs and groups of three would mean that now there were twelve.

Clayton looked away to give his eyes a rest.

When he'd first come to the cabin he kept track of the days by crossing them out on the calendar. Clayton still kept track by crossing out the days as they passed, though he wasn't confident his count was accurate as the days dissolved into nights and nights became days and sometimes he questioned whether he crossed days off too frequently or not frequently enough as it was impossible to *really* tell how long he'd been locked in the cabin.

A gust of wind hammered the window and Clayton jumped.

Had one of the Shrub people thrown a snowball at the window, he questioned.

"No," Clayton said, out loud, though he didn't realize it. "Shrub people have no arms to throw with."

The day beside the last crossed out day on the calendar was Friday. The unmarked square claimed the date was Friday the 17th. March. Clayton was thankful it wasn't Friday the 13th, even though he'd never been superstitious. Friday the 17th was just a regular day. Clayton thought about flipping forward through the calendar to see when the next Friday the 13th was. He thought about flipping the calendar back to determine when the last Friday the 13th happened. He thought about these things until the thoughts passed.

What if one of the Shrub people *did* throw a snowball at the window, Clayton wondered.

This was the first time Clayton had wondered anything in months. He'd thought things. He'd imagined things. He counted things, but Clayton never wondered and only knew he was wondering now by the foreign feeling he felt. Wonder felt the way possibility feels. Not possibility like 'all things are possible with God' possibility; possibility like when you've exhausted all other resources and suddenly discover an option you'd never thought of before that just might work.

Wonder felt like this.

Through the snow he saw that the Shrubs had formed a row like kids did in the school yard playing whatever it was kids played in school yards. In the space between the snowflakes, Clayton thought he heard chanting.

"Red Rover, Red Rover, we call Clayton over. Red Rover, Red Rover, *we* call Clayton over."

He was surprised the Shrubs knew his name. He'd never been outside the cabin since he'd arrived, so Clayton had never introduced himself. Still, the chant continued; Clayton was sure of it. The Shrubs were calling *him* over.

"Red Rover, Red Rover, we call Clayton over."

Clayton felt a warm feeling in his chest. The warm feeling was his heart filling with joy.

"They want me," he said aloud. Whether he was uncaring or unaware is unclear; Clayton repeated the words again out loud for his own ears to hear, "They want me."

Like a puppy hearing the word 'walk,' Clayton wagged his head side-to-side, looking. He didn't know what he was looking for, only that looking seemed the appropriate thing to do.

A burlap sack hung on the hook on the back of the cabin door. If the burlap sack had been a trench coat, where the belt would have hung around the waist, twine was strung across the sack. Twine like the Shrub people had wrapped around their Shrub waists. Clayton questioned briefly why he hadn't noticed the outfit earlier.

"It doesn't matter," he said out loud. "I noticed now."

Clayton didn't like to fret over things like most people did.

Standing up from his seat at the window, he undressed in place then walked naked to the door where the burlap sack hung from its hook. Clayton ran his hand across the material. Burlap was much softer than he had imagined. This caused him to think maybe Friars didn't wear burlap because they were poor, rather for the way the material felt when worn against their skin.

Clayton smiled his first smile in a long time.

The snow was still falling.

The camera still blinked.

Clayton had forgotten both these details.

The Shrub people had called him by name.

"They called me," Clayton said again as he pulled the burlap sack over his head and tightened the twine around his waist.

He walked back to the window and looked out, hoping to see the Shrub people still standing in a line, still calling his name.

In the space between the falling snowflakes, Clayton listened hoping to hear the chant being chanted.

Outside the window was white and if Clayton would have been outside at that moment he would have had difficulty seeing his hand held in front of his face; the snow was that blinding. The Shrubs couldn't be seen. The chant was silenced by the wall of snow.

Of course he couldn't hear the chant, Clayton rationalized. Who could hear anything in this chaos?

"Yes, who indeed," he said out loud.

To Clayton the snow was noise. He heard the static of an old television, hushing and swooshing and creeshing all at once, and thought the snow outside looked like an old television set with nothing but static displayed on the screen; only whiter.

Clayton thought about how long it had taken him to dress. He thought about how long he'd been staring at the white outside and instead of thinking, he walked over to the refrigerator and crossed out another day.

It was now Saturday, March 18th.

In the corner of the square marked eighteen was a hollow circle indicating a full moon.

Doesn't matter, Clayton thought. Can't see the moon anyhow.

Clayton had forgotten the camera, as he sometimes did, until its blinking light caught the corner of his eye. He tilted his head toward the ceiling. Clayton smiled at the thought of how he must look wearing a burlap sack and wondered if the person on the other side, he wondered *if the people on the other side*, thought he looked like a Friar as he thought the Shrubs had, and if they too had pictured him as a Friar going door-to-door like the Jehovah's Witness did in his home town, peddling whatever it was Jehovah's peddled on their trips door-to-door. Clayton wondered if whoever was watching thought as he had thought that burlap was rough and uncomfortable, and then he wondered if whoever they were would ever have the opportunity to wear burlap and discover how soft it actually felt against the skin.

This intense moment of wonder didn't feel like the possibility wonder he'd felt earlier. This time, as Clayton wondered, he felt wonder like how when you look at someone

8

doing something you never thought to do before, how as you watched you decided to try, and by trying, discovered that there was indeed pleasure where you were convinced no pleasure could have existed. Clayton thought about the first time he tried sushi. That kind of wonder.

Clayton smiled a third time and went back to the window. The snow had stopped blowing and was now falling as it had when the Shrub people first called him to join their game. He squinted trying to focus his eyes through the snow. As he squinted he tilted his head to listen closer. In the distance he counted eleven shadows. At first spotting the shadows, before he was certain their identity, Clayton doubted himself because the Shrubs were no longer lined up. Because they were no longer standing in a line, Clayton assumed they had stopped playing their game. This thought disturbed him because if the Shrub people had stopped playing their game maybe they changed their mind about inviting him out, also. As he thought this unsettling thought, and before he could sit down, Clayton heard one of the smaller Shrubs call.

"C-L-A-Y-T-O-N…"

He looked harder out the window. Clayton listened closer. The Shrub people were standing around their barrel, fire burning. He knew this was his chance.

Clayton started toward the cabin door and for the first time since he decided to join the Shrub people, he thought whether the door would be unlocked and if it wasn't how he would open it. Instead of allowing this thought to grow into worry, he tried the handle.

The handle turned.

The turning handle caused Clayton to wonder if the door had ever been locked to begin with. The wonder like how

9

other people fretted over how things could have been if they'd only known sooner or if they'd not found out as soon as they had. Clayton did not enjoy this type of wonder and dismissed the feeling immediately.

A cold gust of wind greeted Clayton as he opened the door. In the distance, through the falling snow, he could see a faint flame burning in the in middle of the shadows.

Without hesitation, as Clayton understood the benefit of never hesitating and always daring, he stepped out of the cabin and into the night to join the friends he knew had called.

BREWERS LAKE

If you take the time to look at a tree as the wind begins to blow you'll observe a metamorphosis. The green leaves fade into silver as the wind forces their under exposed sides toward the sun. Then the wind stills and in an instant the leaves are green again. These trees aren't like that. Across the lake are pines, and if not, some sort of coniferous variation. The sun shines and the wind blows but these trees don't have leaves to dance. Their needles are heavy and their branches hang limp. Gravity is a bitch. It's always pulling you down; no chance of anything but to remain firmly planted on the ground. It's a wonder why we ever choose these trees to decorate at Christmas, but then again, they're perfect. Like these weighted down trees we're all just sad. That's not accurate. We're numb; at least I'm numb. We put on distractions; our ornaments. We top it off with a star; our greatest achievement. Then we position ourselves so everybody can comment about what a nice tree we have. Somewhere along this journey we've tried so hard to become someone else that we've forgotten who we are.

Tilting my head to the right, I look in the eyes of my fiancée. Eye contact is important. This entire time she's been watching me stare across the water, away in my thoughts. She knows I'm happiest in here. My mind. There's a light grin on my face and she's relieved. She worries about me, you know? She admires my ability to go deep but is reluctant to accept the dark passengers that accompany this gift. My smile is perceived that everything is okay.

My gift to her.

I take her by the hand and ask her to jump. She's taken aback; we're fully clothed. I tell her on the count of three. It's always on the count of three.

The water, dark as it is, feels light around the body.

Weightless. The temperature of the water and the temperature of my body interact and exchange without judgement. The water accepts me. The highway traffic that was audible above is silenced. There is no need for conversation down here. Why disrupt the unspoken bliss?

If you hold your breath long enough fear begins to set in. Don't be afraid. What would it be like to stay under here forever, to invite water into my lungs like this water invited me in? Calm. I attempt to breathe and somehow draw in air. Surprised, I open my eyes and there it was: a gift from God. The sun shone above and its ray penetrated down to the lake's bottom, or somewhere near. Beneath the spotlight, I saw it: an anchor. And it's perfect.

Resurfacing, I glow, breaking the water with my face. I start laughing. Liz laughs too; albeit for different reasons. I let her keep that also. We splash around offering sweet nothings in each other's ears. This means the world to her. Atop the embankment and behind the carpark railing, restless travellers who have pulled over for a stretch are snapping pictures of us. Everyone is always trying to capture the moment. Everyone wants to live vicariously through everybody else. I don't protest. Liz gets embarrassed when I lure people into philosophical conversation. It's safer to talk about the weather and what we do for a living. Besides, we're in a National Park; best not scare away the natives.

I figure why have a conversation if it's not about something that will force our minds beyond the natural? People can't honestly be happy working nine-to-five in order to amass some petty fortune. What happens when they're finished? Start to live?

We swim ashore and change into dry clothes for the

duration of our drive home. We have clothes to change into because we're returning from an out-of-town wedding, when like the other restless travellers, we pulled over to stretch.

It's exhausting pretending to fit into another's version of happy. I'd just spent the weekend kissing babies and shaking hands. If I had the time I could probably be a politician. But I don't understand happy people. Happiness has never really appealed to me. I was always the take a couple hits of ecstasy and listen to hospital recordings through my headphones kind of guy. I find beauty in paradox. I think it's the should-be purpose of conversation: to force a mind beyond the natural into the supernatural. Like religion, happiness is a crutch. Or, maybe, more accurately, happiness is a hindrance.

We giggle packing our luggage and resume our course down the highway. This is a welcome reprieve after months of tension. We're creating memories and redeeming ones thought lost.

That anchor. It's perfect. Above water gravity pins you down. But down there, in heaven, you're weightless, and the validity for gravity begins to build its case. If you want to breathe water forever, you'd need to develop a simulation for that otherwise oppressive force.

I reach over and take her hand. I tell her this has been the most fun I've had in a while and give her a gentle squeeze. When we arrive home we unpack. I pour each of us a glass a wine. It's wine from the weekend preceding the one we just returned from. We're always doing something.

Retiring to the veranda, it's deceivingly bright for half past eight. We're listening to the wind-chimes compose a sonata. There's a robin dancing playfully through the sprinkler's mist. I smile. Watching the birds frolic about always makes me smile.

They're so innocent and uninterested in the things we busy ourselves with. Sometimes a butterfly will join their fun. My fiancée comments how wonderful it was to share today and I suggest we make a day of it the following weekend. We'll picnic by the lake before a swim. She leans over and nudges me for a kiss.

Fastening myself to the anchor won't be difficult. I learned knots in boy scouts. A simple snare will perform eloquently. No need to complicate things. I'll have to use a type of line instead of rope in order to conceal it in my swim trunks. One end will be tied off with a loop to act as the slip knot. The other end will be tied in the snare. After I dive into the water, I'll only have to complete a couple tasks. First, to thread the loop through the eye of the anchor, followed by, running the snared end through the loop. Then I'll just slip my foot through the snare. The beauty of this knot is that it tightens under load. The greater the tension, the tighter it becomes. I won't be able to struggle free or untie it should I wish to retreat from this breathtaking experience.

Interestingly enough, knowing the definitive moment at which I'll stage my farewell has a way of making everything else a little more bearable.

THE GLADIATOR

"Thank you for flying United Airlines," the stewardess said with a smile. "Enjoy the rest of your trip."

Raymond made eye contact with the blonde and said, "Thank you," but thought, *I would eat your pussy until you screamed.* He thought, *shit, I'd eat your sweaty asshole after a bike ride on a hot day.*

On a full flight of a hundred passengers it seemed Rachel had spent a great deal of time checking on Ray, making conversation with Ray, smiling at Ray. It may have all been in Raymond's head that he was receiving special attention from this young lady but it didn't matter. For most of the flight Raymond had sat with a half-chub in his pants, hoping to catch her glance at him as she entered the lavatory. Raymond was ready to follow her through the unlocked door. He'd heard of the women who take to flight regularly, how they leave the lavatory door unlocked, skirts hiked up and seated on the sink fingering themselves, waiting for a man to stumble in and fuck her at thirty thousand feet. Raymond thought Rachel might have been one of these women. Of course it didn't happen. Not that Raymond was a repulsive middle-aged man. If you can call thirty middle-aged. Ray was fit, clean cut, and relatively successful running his own recycling company. Married and childless, some might even call him a prize. But.

Raymond never followed Rachel through the lavatory door simply because he hadn't observed Rachel enter the lavatory.

Walking up the ramp to the terminal he wondered who had been sent to pick him up. Raymond's rule was if a young lady, attractive or not, was holding the sign with his name on it, he'd remove his wedding band as he descended the escalator before acknowledging her. Ever since Women's Lib became the rule instead of the exception it took a lot more energy to turn a girl while wearing a wedding ring. It used to be so that when a woman saw the gold on a man's ring finger it was a magnet. Now, not so much.

Two university aged girls were standing side-by-side, smiling, holding a white sheet of paper with Mr. Hall printed in bold black letters. Like Raymond had done so many times before, he slipped his solitary gold band into his pants pocket then waved to the girls.

"Good afternoon, ladies," Ray said as he walked toward them.

"Good afternoon, Mr. Hall," they said in a type of unison that would have creeped Ray out if he'd ever seen The Shining, but he hadn't. "How was your flight?"

Before Ray answered he was picturing a threesome. He was imagining stacking the girls on top each other and slipping from one hole to the other as he licked the tits of the brunette.

"Flawless flight," Raymond said. "I've never had any problems flying United."

"That's great to hear, Mr. Hall, do you–"

"Please, call me Ray."

The girl who had started talking, the blonde, Cindy, pursed her lips. It appeared she was deciding whether it was appropriate to accept his urging. Ray imagined he'd see this facial expression again as she knelt before him about to swallow his load.

"Okay, Ray," Cindy said. "Do you have any luggage to collect?"

"Just what I'm carrying," Ray said. "I'm only here for the conference and back home tomorrow."

"That's easy," Jessica said.

Raymond thought, *isn't it?*, and felt the blood begin to flow to his center, producing the same half-chub he sported the duration of the flight.

"We're parked right out front," Jessica said.

"Great."

Jessica drove a black Cadillac Escalade which was far too big for a girl of her size and would have conflicted with Raymond's green business morals if Raymond had morals of any sort. Cindy opened the door for Ray. Raymond basked in the service. He tossed his bag onto the seat and climbed in. To his surprise, Cindy followed and closed the door behind her.

This is going to be easier than I thought.

As the Cadillac pulled away from the curb and out of temporary parking, a Lincoln Town car pulled into the newly vacant spot. The driver activated his hazard lights and rushed into the airport, obviously late, with his own placard for his arriving guest. Printed in bold black letters on the white sheet was *Mr. R. Hall.*

"Are you going straight to the conference centre, Mr.–*Ray,*" Jessica said into the rear view mirror, "or should we stop by the hotel first?"

Raymond couldn't believe his ears. *These girls are down to fuck.*

"Let's stop by the hotel first," Raymond said. "Maybe we'll even have time for a quick drink."

The girls smiled.

Resting her hand on Raymond's leg, Cindy said, "Only if you don't tell anybody."

"I won't if you don't."

Cindy left her hand rested in place. Occasionally she applied just an ever so noticeable amount of pressure. A couple times she slowly ran her hand down toward his knee and back up to his groin. Jessica pulled the Cadillac into the drop-off laneway of the hotel and parked.

"I think, just to be safe" Jessica said, "I'll park in the lot out back and after you check-in, you can let us in from there."

In all my years, Raymond thought then said, "That is a very professional idea, Jessica. Let's do that."

Grabbing his bag and exiting the vehicle, Jessica pulled away. Raymond entered the lobby grinning. He checked himself into the hotel. On his way to the parking lot's access door, he stopped by the boutique and bought a bottle of rum and a litre of cola. The conference wasn't scheduled to begin for another three hours, plenty of time for a couple drinks and some good old fashioned promiscuity.

Both girls were waiting at the side entrance. Raymond let them in and they walked giddily to the elevator. With the elevator doors closed and ascending, in a voice you'd expect from a freshman girl attending her first wet t-shirt contest, Cindy said, "This is sooo bad."

Jessica added, "I can't believe we're doing this."

Raymond smiled, "I never would have imagined."

This, of course, was a lie.

Slipping the plastic card into the slide on room 537, the green light blinked and Ray opened the door. Almost instantly Cindy was smothering him. She pressed him against the wall, kissed his neck and kissed his mouth. Jessica took Ray's bag and the liquor and poured three drinks. If Raymond hadn't been preoccupied by his assumed dream-come-true, he would have seen Jessica dissolve two white tablets into his drink.

"Cindy, my god," Jessica said playfully. "You don't waste any time."

Between kisses, Cindy replied, "We don't have much time, Jess."

"Well, I need a drink before I do anything," Jessica said, holding up two glasses of rum and Coke.

"I'll second that," Raymond said and gestured for one of the drinks Jessica held.

Cindy smiled. She pulled off her top and exposed a black bra cupping juvenile tits.

"Cheers to that," Raymond said. He gulped his drink back and began unbuttoning his shirt.

Jessica turned on the television, "Let's have something on in the background. We might get a little noisy."

"Who are you girls?" Raymond chuckled out loud.

"Just two girls who know what they want," Cindy said.

That was the last thing Raymond remembered hearing.

Raymond woke with his mouth taped. His arms were stretched out on either side and were tied to the bed posts. His feet were bound together and when the cleaning staff would find his body, they'd find the resemblance to Jesus on the Cross quite disturbing.

On the television, Russel Crow was walking into an arena of spectators, ready to fight, *Gladiator* style.

On the nightstand beside the bed was Raymond's solitary gold wedding band.

"You know what I like most about Gladiators?" Jessica said.

If Raymond could have responded, he probably wouldn't have. Jessica's question was rhetorical. She only paused to make sure she had Ray's undivided attention.

Both girls were fully clothed.

"The longer a Gladiator fights," Jessica said, then repeated, "The longer a Gladiator fights, the more likely it is he will die." She smiled. "You've been doing this a long time." Another pause. Jessica could be very dramatic when she wanted to be. "Haven't you, Ray?"

Cindy ripped the Duct-Tape from Ray's face. The rip felt like Cindy had torn a strip of his skin, but it was only the tape. For now.

"You girls have it all wrong," Ray said pleadingly.

Jessica ignored him. "You had to know at some point you'd get caught."

Ray didn't respond.

"You're poor wife," Cindy added. "You know, if you'd just left your ring on when you came down that escalator none of this would be happening."

Ray glared at Cindy.

"She's right, Ray." Jessica said. "Your wife is such a gracious woman, I wanted to do this either way but she was adamant, only if you took your ring off."

"You took your ring off Ray." Cindy said.

Raymond felt beads of sweat forming on his forehead. "I have money," he said.

"Oh, Ray," Jessica said. "You don't."

"That pretty little wife of yours, well, you share a bank account. She gave us your money already," Cindy said.

"If we'd believed her how much of a dirt-bag you really were, Ray, we would have done this pro-bono, wouldn't we have, Cin."

Cindy nodded.

"But here we are," Jessica continued. "And it would seem that you don't have a leg to stand on."

Despite the seriousness of the situation, Raymond felt himself becoming hard. Something about the girls being dominating aroused him.

The things I would let you do to me, Raymond thought, not daring to speak.

His erect penis spoke volumes.

"Hey Cindy," Jessica said. "Would you look at this?"

Jessica nodded toward Raymond's lifted cock.

"A real dirt-bag to the end, don't you think?"

"I dunno. I think we should give him one last throw? I mean, I'm kinda turned on by all of this."

"I don't see why not," Jessica said, "No need to punish ourselves for his crimes."

It took all of Raymond's willpower to keep his lips from forming a grin. *Jesus*, he thought.

Cindy tore a piece of tape from the roll and stretched it across Raymond's face.

"I don't want to hear him speak, though," she said. "Might kill the mood."

She lied. She didn't want anybody to hear him scream.

Cindy stripped and climbed on top of Ray. She pumped her hips, grinding the lips of her vagina along his shaft. Jessica watched. Cindy really was wet from all of this and left a film of shine on Raymond's cock.

"Pass me a condom, will ya, Jess?" Cindy said. "Don't want this sleaze bag knocking me up, or god forbid, giving me the clap. Who knows where he's been."

Raymond was staring at the shaved lips on either side of his dick. If he could have bit his lips, he would have. Raymond truly had a one track mind. He didn't see Jessica pass Cindy a box cutter. If he had, he would have started squirming. Raymond was too fixated on the warmth pouring from Cindy's cunt to notice anything.

Cindy ran her free hand over his penis while sliding her body further down his bound legs.

Gripping his cock in one hand and reaching forward with the other, Cindy paused just long enough for Raymond to glimpse the sharp object she wielded. Before he could register what she was doing Cindy thrust the blade through the base of his erect flesh and cut wildly until she'd cut right through. It was not a clean cut. Blood squirted like jizz from the quarter sized hole where Raymond's prized penis had previously stood at attention. His body thrashed uncontrollably. There was a moment the girls thought he might break free from the restraints, but like all moments, it was fleeting. Ray's eyes rolled in his head so that only white could be seen. Back and neck arched, Raymond's entire body flexed. His screams remained muffled. The girls weren't expecting such a show. Most guys just stared in disbelief before passing out. Raymond looked possessed.

Finally, his body limped onto the blood soaked sheets.

Cindy walked calmly to the bathroom and tossed the slab of flesh into the toilet.

"Would you like to do the honors?" Cindy asked.

"Go ahead Cin. I'll do the next one."

Cindy pressed the lever on the tank and watched Raymond's penis spiral down the bowl before disappearing to wherever penises disappear to when flushed down a toilet.

DATING ONLINE

It was as if he was peeling a banana, the man's skin separated as he pulled a barber's razor across his chest. Like unzipping a fat man's jacket or fingering the slit of a cunt. Not immediately, but almost so, blood began to pour from the wound and run down his stomach. Starting just below the collarbone he dragged the razor to his naval, intersecting the first cut to make a bloody 't'.

The man stood staring at the mirror watching the blood flow from his work. Surprisingly, the cutting did not hurt. He wondered if what came next would. The man took the razor and carefully cut circles around his nipples to ensure they remained in place.

Picking at the 't' in the center of his chest, he peeled up a corner and began pulling the skin away. The sound of skin pulling from his muscle was the sound of a laminate sheet pulling from a piece of paper. Immediately the man felt pain but he did not stop until he had pulled the skin to the end of the cuts and allowed the flap to hang freely.

He looked like a painting, the man thought, observing his art in the mirror. Where the nipple had been was a hole in the free hanging flap. He was thankful for this. He didn't know what would happen if he'd pulled off a nipple and didn't want to find out.

Returning to the 't' in the center of his chest he picked at the next corner and began to peel back his skin as he did the first. The pain felt like peeling a Band-Aid that had been secured far past when it needed to be, but he refused to relent. He was determined.

Two sections of skin hung from his belly. Two sections remained.

When the man was younger, a teenager, he remembered

the experience of getting his first tattoo. The initial pain of the needle penetrating his skin at a hundred piercings a second stung, but shortly after the tattoo artist began, he became numb to the pain. He even began to enjoy it. Not until the needle passed over his shinbone did the pain become so acute that when the tattooist finished the first piece, the young man stopped him from mirroring the barbs on his opposite leg. He remembered making the excuse that it would be more artistic to leave the band on only one of his ankles, that everybody always got both sides tattooed simultaneously. The tattoo artist knew it was a lie but humoured the young man so not to insult his adolescent pride.

Staring in the mirror watching blood pebble on the now exposed muscle, the man wondered if he would stop peeling as he had stopped that tattoo all those years back.

No, he stated firmly. He would finish.

Securing a corner between his forefinger and thumb, he pulled quicker than he had the first two and twisted his face at the spike in pain. He thought about leaving the last patch of skin in place. He began to rationalize like everybody does when attempting to justify whatever behaviour they're hoping to justify. He started to shake. Nausea struck and the man felt faint. He balanced himself on the sink. He closed his eyes to preserve whatever strength he had left.

A knock on the bathroom door jarred him from his concentration.

"Jerry," the woman's voice said. "Is everything okay in there?"

The man opened his eyes and calmly replied, "Oh yeah, sorry, I'll be out in a second."

Pushing his fingers into the muscles on his chest he fit

two under the last patch of skin. Annoyed by the interruption, he ripped his hand back and tore the skin past the razor cuts, up toward his shoulder. He gritted his teeth and let out a grunt.

Testosterone surged through his body. His adrenaline surged. Eyes wide and staring at himself in the mirror, he smiled a joker's grin.

Yeah, everything is just perfect in here.

The sink was smeared with blood, as was the floor where he stood. Specs of blood had struck the mirror and could be seen on the ceiling from when he yanked at the last corner of skin. His hands were covered in red.

The man whom the woman called Jerry was not Jerry the elementary school teacher she had met online. Jerry was the name he used to troll dating sites.

Tonight was the first time they'd met.

Unmistakeably, it would be their last.

Shirtless, opened, and bloody, the man exited the bathroom and rejoined his date in her living room. The woman was sitting on the couch scrolling through the titles on Netflix.

"I was thinking we could watch that new Bruce Willis movie that came out, what do you think?" The man placed his hands gently on her shoulders. As girls do in moments of sensuality she shut her eyes and tilted her head back. She rubbed his hand with the side of her face.

His hands were viscous.

The woman opened her eyes.

She screamed.

The man clasped his hands around her neck, obstructing the air's attempted escape. He forced her flat on the couch and sat on top of her.

"I'm going to loosen my grip," the man started. "If you

scream again, I'll kill you where you lay."

The woman stared up at him with terror filled eyes.

Only an hour earlier they'd shared a meal they'd prepared together. During dinner he'd spoken so sincerely the woman was sure she'd finally met a man she could trust.

For a month leading up to this night, Jerry and her had carried a daily conversation through email and on the phone. She wanted a relationship built on communication rather than sex. Jerry had respected that. He respected her. He treated her as if she was the only girl in the world and never pressured her to get together or complained about how long they'd been talking without having ever met. He seemed like the perfect guy. All of this flashed in her mind as the man held her down, skin hanging from his torso, and blood dripping on her blouse.

"Do you understand me," the man said.

The woman nodded as much as she could nod with two hands gripping her neck.

He stared a deep stare which violated her soul. The woman felt dirty. The man slowly released his grip though remained perched atop her.

He held the sides of her face as one would prior to moving in for a kiss. A gesture romantic in every other setting but this. The woman trembled.

Sliding down her body, he pulled her to seated and began forcing her head toward his center. A gesture similar to when a man is guiding a woman toward fellatio. A blowjob is not what this man was after.

"Lick the flaps," the man commanded.

He held her head close to his chest. The hanging skin brushed the sides of the woman's face. She shook her head but did not speak.

"Lick the flaps," the man repeated forcing her head closer to his exposed and bleeding muscles.

The woman's lips were sealed in defiance. The man pulled her hair back and struck her face.

"It's not a suggestion," he glared.

The woman tried to look away but he pulled her hair tighter into compliance.

"Stick your tongue out."

The tears streaming from the woman's eyes mixed with the man's blood on her cheeks and became a heavily applied layer of blush a ballet dancer would wear. The woman slowly pushed her tongue through her lips. The man pulled her head toward him again.

"Lick."

The woman pressed her tongue to one of the hanging sections of skin as a child might lick a metal pole in the school yard when dared to by friends. Just the tip of her tongue.

"Lick!"

She started wiggling her tongue as he guided her head up and down and side to side. The man wasn't sure if he'd be able to feel the touch of her tongue on the peeled skin. He focussed on the experience. Eventually he displayed a surprised grin at the tickling sensation. He felt himself become erect and debated raping the woman.

Too cliché, the man thought, dismissing the urge.

After several minutes of tonguing, the man released his hold over the woman's head and allowed her to stop. Blood covered her lips and chin. The woman's tears had nearly washed away the blood from her cheeks. She laid back sobbing.

"You did good, kiddo," the man said with a smile.

He patted her face.

"We should do this again sometime."

DOWNTOWN

Entering the men's room he didn't expect it to smell like a woman, but it did. The scent was black with tight braided hair and daddy on her lips. Around the corner was stale beer and dehydrated piss. One hand for stabilizing the other for aim, his dick burned under pressure. Unconcerned, he shook it off as he recalled his friend's admonition how he never worried about burning because for as long as he remembered whenever he pushed too hard his dick burned, too. Forcing this piss before the bathroom attendant setup his station meant not having to pay a dollar to wash his hands. Tossing the paper towel into the trash he looked in the mirror and said, "Like anybody needs help washing their fucking hands."

OFF-PEAK

Mary was the lady who always sat near the window. Today she was wearing a blue dress with her resting disheveled smile.

"Did last night's power outage affect you?" she asked the lady sitting across from her.

"Do you know what happened?" the lady said.

"It was a planned power outage. Hydro had to trim the trees around the lines," Mary answered.

"No. I knew that," the lady said. "I meant to me."

"I didn't know Hydro still trimmed the trees around the power lines," Sue said. Sue was always late to the conversation. Most times she simply ooed and nodded like a Pentecostal on Sundays.

"Hydro takes care of the trees around their lines," Mary said. "Town is powered by Local Hydro and they're the ones who hire arborists instead of doing it themselves."

"I wonder why that is?" Sue said. "Maybe they don't have the staffing anymore."

The lady across from Mary began again, "I knew about the power going out, but I forgot to set my alarm before I went to bed."

"Ooo," Sue said.

"I woke in the middle of the night and had to feel my way through the dark to the kitchen to set the wind-up clock I keep in the drawer."

"It's a good thing you woke up and remembered," Sue said.

"I've seen Local Hydro cutting trees in town, Mary," the lady said. "The day before last I called Dick over to look at the boy in the bucket. I said, 'the boy's just a kid,' but Dick didn't think so."

"Well maybe if it's an emergency Local Hydro will do it,"

Mary said.

"I don't know," the lady across from her said. "When they were working farther down the street it was a man in the bucket, not a boy."

"Must be the harder cuts the man does and the easier ones the boy does," Sue said.

"They must think with us staring at them through the window we have nothing better to do," the lady across from Mary said.

"What do they expect if we can't do our laundry until after 7 p.m.?"

Sue nodded.

PARALLELS

Everybody was always telling Henry what he should do. They were telling him what he thought. They were always telling him something. Nobody listened. If people would have listened maybe Henry would have felt different, but they never did and Henry always felt the same: alone. Despite people always being around, his loneliness was the only thing to keep him company.

"Henry," the lady said as she opened the waiting room door. "I wasn't expecting you."

Henry gave the lady a quizzical look, then questioned (to himself) the date and time. It was Wednesday. It was three o'clock in the afternoon. He wondered what she meant that she wasn't expecting him.

"I was expecting someone of the different sex," the lady qualified.

Earlier that morning Henry had contemplated the idea of having a vagina instead of a penis, what it would feel like to have his vagina entered into by a penis, and wondered if it would hurt or if it would feel as good or even better than having a penis and penetrating a vagina.

He asserted, surely the lady couldn't have known he'd contemplated this earlier in the day.

"Come on in, let's check."

Henry followed her into the office. She left the door open because there was no one else in the waiting room.

"It's Wednesday at three," Henry said. "We always meet Wednesday at three."

"I know, but for some reason I have you scratched out," the lady said. "I'm back to back Wednesdays at three."

Henry didn't know what she meant by back-to-back-Wednesdays-at-three so he took a seat on the arm of the chair.

"I have a message here, it's probably the lady I'm supposed to be meeting with. Maybe she's cancelled."

You're supposed to be meeting with me, Henry thought. He tried not to glare.

"Hi Shelley, it's Sabrina," the answering machine started playing.

Henry wondered if Shelley should be listening to her confidential voicemail with a client in the room. He wondered if she'd ever played his messages while someone else was in the room. He'd left some concerning messages in the past and thinking this thought Henry became self-conscience, embarrassed, and slightly betrayed.

"I'm running a few minutes late, I should be there by quarter after."

It was actually three-thirty on Wednesday afternoon, Shelley was late with the last client. Henry thought people must be really fucked up if Shelley has been double booking and running late and decided if people were really all that fucked up he'd give up his appointment time for their sake. They probably needed it more, he rationalized.

He didn't have to decide that because Shelley didn't offer to see him.

"I have an opening at five this evening if you want to wait around," she said. "Do you have anything to do?"

"No," Henry said. "It's okay. Don't worry. I'll see you next time. Next Wednesday at three?"

"Let's check."

Shelley flipped the page in her agenda and shook her head.

"No," I have you scratched out there, too. I wonder what happened?"

"Oh, okay then. The week after. The 20th."

"Okay, yeah, that will work. But if you're free tonight at five, or if you're home by then, we can do a session on the phone."

Henry though about it. He didn't need to. A session on the phone wouldn't feel comfortable. If Shelley was this lax with her confidential voicemail he wondered who would be listening in real time. That and when people talk on the phone, they're never really listening, not that anybody ever really listened anyway; usually they're doodling, or watching T.V., or checking their e-mail, or their calendars, or they're eating.

"No, that's okay, really. Two weeks from now."

Shelley sensed his apprehension. "Do you have FaceTime?"

Henry didn't. He also didn't know what FaceTime was. He assumed something like Skype, but didn't ask. He didn't care.

"No, no. Don't worry. I don't want to have to rush home, the snow storm and all. We'll just meet again next time."

"I feel really bad that you drove all the way here."

"It's okay, I like to drive."

"Okay, then. Thanks, and if you need anything before I see you next, please call. We can talk on the phone."

"Okay, I will," Henry said, but he knew he wouldn't. "Oh. I brought you my book."

He handed her the book he'd just published. She mentioned how she wanted a signed copy when they came in. Henry tended to remember everything. It was a haunting behaviour habit. More so for him. Memories aren't owned. They imprison.

"That's really considerate of you. I still have the copy you sent to the publisher. The one in the red folder."

Henry knew she did and that she hadn't read it. People are always saying they're going to do something when they won't. Lives of lies. Promises for show and never to be kept.

"How are you doing though? Are you okay?"

"Yeah, I'm good."

"Are you sure?"

Henry thought maybe she was trying to cover her ass just in case something happened between now and the next time he saw her. He thought she wanted to be able to say she hadn't noticed anything concerning when he showed up to her office last.

"Yeah," Henry said. "Okay, well, see you next time."

"Drive safe, Henry. It's pretty bad out there."

Henry left the office. He stopped by the men's room before he took the stairs down to the lobby. He paid his parking pass and zipped up his jacket. The wind pelted his face with bits of glass-like snow. With his head tucked low, he walked against the wind to his car and got inside. He turned on the wipers. They were useless. Henry had to get out and scrape the windows despite only being inside for forty minutes.

At the gate he opened the window to insert his ticket and the wind pelted him again. Henry didn't mind the snow. He minded the rain less. Sometimes when it was pouring outside, he'd go for a walk. He'd be drenched after the first couple steps but the warm rain and the sound of the drops striking the pavement, the sensation of the water slapping his face, he enjoyed. The snow was only rain, but colder. Regardless, he rolled up his window, turned up the radio, and drove away.

As Henry drove, he wondered how Shelley would feel if

when he got home, he loaded his shotgun and pulled the trigger with the barrel lodged deep in his throat.

"She'd probably feel pretty shitty," he said to the rear view mirror.

He wondered if she'd feel just as bad if he swallowed a bottle of pills after drinking himself into a stupor or if he'd passed through the kitchen and used the meat cleaver to hack at his wrists and thighs. There had been nights where Henry was too afraid to pass through his kitchen for that very reason.

As Henry was thinking these thoughts, a car swerved into his lane. He'd been watching the car approach in his rear view mirror and slowed down appropriately, anticipating the recklessness. Henry thought about slamming his fist into the horn, but didn't do it. He wished people would learn to drive according to the weather. He thought the real liability on the road were other drivers.

The swerver provoked the thought of getting in the midst of a twenty-car pileup and so he wondered what Shelley would think about him driving all the way to their regularly scheduled appointment, only to drive home two hours in the snow. He smiled thinking she'd feel bad. "She should," he said, not taking his eyes from the road. "She should."

The drive home was long. The music was playing loud, and as the music blared Henry remembered his empty refrigerator. He decided to pull off at the next exit and pick up some groceries so he'd be able to make breakfast in the morning.

In the grocery store he found everything he wanted: bread for toast, cheese to put on the toast, bacon because bacon, eggs because you can't have breakfast without eggs. When Henry went grocery shopping he always brought his own bags;

not because he cared about the environment – Henry didn't give a shit about the environment – but because ever since everybody else started giving a shit about the environment, grocery stores started charging a nickel a bag as guilt tax or something. As he shopped he loaded the items he needed for breakfast into the bags he brought. The first time he did this, he thought maybe people would think he was trying to steal groceries, but when he witnessed someone else doing the same thing he stopped worrying. He didn't usually care what other people thought, at least that's what he told himself, but he did. At least relative to how everyone else who doesn't care what people think about them, think about them.

"Good day, sir," the cashier said. She wore lightly blonde hair in a pony and greeted Henry with a smile.

"Hello," Henry smiled back. Nice people should be greeted nicely.

The lady scanned his items through, "That will be $19.74," she said.

"Visa please," Henry said, his bag already repacked.

"Master Card?" the lady said.

"No, Visa."

How she could confuse the two, Henry did not know.

"I'm sorry, sir, we don't accept Visa. Only Interac and Master Card."

Henry didn't have either. There were people staring at him in front and waiting behind.

"I only have Visa," Henry checked his pockets, "and 18 cents in my pocket."

The cashier stared blankly.

"Can I just leave these things here?" Henry asked.

"Of course," she said.

She seemed annoyed.

He felt like he was being judged.

Henry unloaded the grocery bag he had brought and left the line. He left the groceries he wanted to use for breakfast. He left the people staring. He left the ones biting their embarrassed lips for him. He felt stupid. He felt embarrassed, and as Henry was allowing the feeling of embarrassment to turn his face red, the cold snowy air struck him like a backhand from an accusing lover.

He squinted his way to his car, scraped off the windshield for the second time and drove away.

"Fuck. Fuck. Fuck."

Henry was hitting his steering wheel and screamed one last fuck. This time with mother.

"Mother fuck!"

In spite of his anger, he drove slowly out of the parking lot, which turned out to be a smart move. Another driver, who was in denial of the weather, skidded into his lane and may very well have hit Henry should Henry have been driving according to his mood.

Henry sighed.

Red light.

The longest red light that day. Maybe ever in the history of red lights. When the light turned green Henry pulled into the intersection.

The trucker coming down the overpass was daydreaming; asleep behind the wheel; driving recklessly; secretly a human being with an over aggressive taste for vehicular manslaughter; or simply negligent – which may be worse than all the rest. This trucker hadn't slowed when he crested the hill approaching the light and although he hadn't been in sight when Henry pulled into the intersection, the transport truck was clearly visible now. Henry pressed the accelerator. There was no traction to be had. His tires spun in place. Snow and slush and wet kicked up a cloud all around his car. Henry slammed on his horn knowing even if he got the trucker's attention it would have been too late. He tried to make eye contact with the driver. Again, to no avail. The drivers in the vehicles near the intersection stared in disbelief. When accidents like this happen, everybody always sees them coming, but to be able to see it coming, you have to be frozen in place. Everybody was very frozen.

When asked the question whether someone wants to know when they're going to die, the jury is split. Some people don't want to know while others do. In this moment, Henry knew he was going to die and knowing he was going to die, he smiled. Shelley once told him smiling relaxes every bone in the body.

***

The bathroom fan hums, though it may as well not be. The refrigerator clicks cyclically, though its sound remains muted. With the shades drawn and the lights out and the walls bare the silence is deafening. Outside, cars rush past and horns honk in the race that comprises day-to-day living. Behind the house birds sing, geese quack, and the neighbour dog occasionally barks; none of it enough to break the fog of silence.

That's not entirely true. The thoughts running through his mind are megaphones chanting metronomically. An endless beat of everything he'd ever said. Snare drums sounding everything he'd ever done. A drawn out trumpet blast of everything he should have and could have and would have done if only he knew better at the time. A brass band of regret trouncing the silence in overwhelmingly deafening tones.

How many days has it been like this? How many weeks? Has a month elapsed? He doesn't know. His phone has remained off. The flag on his mailbox has remained erect. His social media has gone the way of New Orleans: wiped out. If someone had been trying to get a hold of him he wouldn't have known. Not that anybody tried to get a hold of him. Before he disconnected, everything had remained silent for days, not that he would have responded to any inquest if someone *had* reached out. As the world turns and its inhabitants go on with their mere life experience, Helm is almost forgotten. At the very least, he's dispensable. He doesn't know which is worse. And it doesn't matter.

They say a rut is a few feet shy of a grave. Helm's rut is probably closer to a foot. Teetering the thread that separates life from non-life, if he were to go this moment nobody would notice for days. At least until his body began to decompose and the excrement he expelled during his final breath had begun to eat through the floor. Only then might the scent draw attention. If he had a cat he might never be discovered. The feline race is known to eat their owners if their owners die unnoticed. Something that would never happen if Helm owned a dog. A dog would lay down beside Helm and cry until it starved to death. Man's best friend for a reason. Regardless, Helm doesn't have a dog or a cat.

The trend these days is the self-development positivity movement. Everybody is special. Everybody matters. Here's a trophy for showing up. You're important. Anybody who's anybody knows this is a bullshit trend. The only common denominator that connects all of humanity is pain. Maybe pain and suffering. Sure, everybody is drawn to an inspiring story – if it's possible for them, it's possible for me – but that's not true either. It's voyeurism. It's a distraction from one's own existence. Then again, it's only subconscious because who has time these days to contemplate the larger questions in life? Nobody. Everybody getting up, going to work, coming home, eating, flopping onto the couch with a drink and the remote to forget their day by watching the *reality* of someone else's. Going to bed, waking up, and doing it all over again. Every day from kindergarten to retirement. Only the lucky ones get snuffed out somewhere in between. Better still to have never been born. Otherwise they work their entire lives, all of their best years behind them, to one day withdraw from everything they ever held close into retirement with their health declining and waiting out the sweet reprieve that is death. But nobody acknowledges this, but if they do they're quickly dismissed or chastised or medicated. The trend today is positivity. Everything is possible. And if you're eating gluten and not supporting refugees or not shopping fair trade, you're evil. Depressed? Do you know how good you have it in North America? You're among the 1% of the wealthiest people on earth. Did you know that most of the world lives on $1 a day? You don't see them lamenting the bane of their existence. You're such a solipsist. The world doesn't revolve around you. And on and on and on until you give the extra dollar with each purchase to whichever fund is all the rave. To whatever fund they're pressuring you for. Why does it have to be this way?

For a moment, the brass band stops playing and Helm remembers a story.

There once was a man. A man of modest means who lived by the sea. This man had married the lady he loved and together they had a child. Living by the sea with his wife and young child they were happy. Each morning the man would rise from his slumber, kiss his wife good morning and make coffee. He'd then pack his lunch and head toward the water to fish, as fishing is how he earned his modest income, and more importantly, fed his family. In the afternoon when the sun was highest in the sky and hottest on the ground, he'd return to shore with his catch, deposit most with the fish salesmen at the pier, then return home with dinner. In the evenings they'd eat as a family and drink wine and sit under the stars enjoying each other's presence before retiring for the evening to make love and fall asleep in warm embrace. The man and his wife, they lived a simple life; but what is life more than eating and drinking and making love?

One day, as the story always goes, a foreigner came to the small fishing village and observed the man and his daily routine. The foreigner was impressed with the man's discipline and work ethic, so he pulled him aside one afternoon as he returned to shore with his catch.

"Sir," the foreigner said, introducing himself as a business man from America. "I've observed you and your work and I'm impressed."

The man did not know how to respond as he was not working to impress another, simply working to return home to his wife.

The foreigner continued. "With your experience and discipline it would be fairly easy to purchase several other fishing boats and arrange a fleet of fishermen to go out with you each morning."

"Why would I want to do that?" the man replied.

"Well, to earn more."

"I don't need to earn more, my family is taken care of and we are happy."

"Yes, I can see that," the foreigner said. "But if you'd just hear me out it will only take a minute."

The man didn't respond, and the foreigner, as foreigners often do, mistook the man's politeness for approval.

"If you were to arrange a fleet of fishermen to go with you each day your catch would be multiplied duly. Over time you'd be able to purchase more boats and hire more fisherman, building a strong fleet to capitalize on. With the surplus catch you'd be able to set up a distribution center and sell your fish abroad for great profits. If you would stick with this long enough, eventually you'd be able to take your company public and sell it for millions of dollars."

The man interrupted. "I don't need millions of dollars."

"No, you may not think so, but if you did all of this you'd be able to retire and then you'd be able to spend all your days with you wife and son, and you'd never have to work again."

"Sir, how long would all of what you just described take to accomplish?"

"Oh, I'm going to be straight with you. It will be hard work. You'll have to work long days and late nights while you're building everything and you will most certainly encounter many hardships along the way, but if I was to give you a conservative estimate, there are people who have pulled similar feats off in no less than 30 years."

The man smiled.

The foreigner interpreted this as acceptance.

The foreigner was wrong.

"Thirty years of hard labour, away from my wife, missing my son grow up," the man paused. "Thirty years of this in hopes of selling the company so that I can retire?"

"Your family would admire your accomplishments and would serve as an excellent foundation for your son to look up to."

"Thirty years of this to settle down into a quiet lifestyle, living by the sea with my wife, living simply?"

"Isn't it beautiful?"

"I have this now. Why would I waste these precious thirty years ahead of me to come full circle?"

The foreigner stared at him blankly.

"In the mornings I rise with my wife and we have coffee before I set out to sea. In the afternoon I return with our dinner and some extra money from the extra fish I caught. In the evening we eat heartily, drink deeply, and make love before falling asleep in each other's arms," the man said, eyes looking through the foreigner in reminiscence. "I have all that I desire, and if you'll excuse me, I have my family to return to."

The man bowed his head in exit and left the foreigner speechless where he stood. The foreigner had never thought of life in this way. He had always thought one must grow up, consuming, progressing, and expanding; working hard to live a retired life. Never had he thought it possible to live that life, now.

Obviously it was possible. The man had just described something wonderful.

A wave crashed against the shore. Its reprieve pulled rocks into contact with each other as the water sucked back into the sea. The thought escaped the foreigner, and he shook

his head smiling, "Uneducated fool. He could have so much."
Then he left the village and proceeded to the next.

The thing about wanting what you have.

Life could be so simple.

Eating and drinking and making love.

The bass started again. The snare kicked in, but before the trumpet could blast, Helm slapped himself across his face. The slap was so hard it left a print as the blood below the surface of the skin quickly rose. He shook away the pain. He shook away the brass band. He used his other hand and slapped the other side of his face. This time not as hard, though equally refreshing; something about balance.

Outside the dark walls of his lightless home he could hear the cars rushing by. He could hear the birds chirping out back and the occasional dog bark from next door. Helm stood up, ripped open the curtains. He moved through each room and pulled all the drawstrings on each of the blinds. Light poured in like blood gushing from a wound. He winced at the brightness. He went to the front door and opened it wide. He went to the back door and did the same. The air from outside vanquished the stale scent of *rut*. Bright light. Fresh air. Rosy cheeks. Helm stood tall and looked around his home.

Helm thought about the man in the proverb. He thought about each morning how he'd get up and head out to sea. He thought about how the boat traversed the water and the wake it left behind. When he thought about the wake he thought about how the wake doesn't steer the boat. He thought about all of his regrets. He thought about everything he'd ever said and everything he'd ever done, and how if he'd known better at the time, he would have done better. And then Helm thought his reflecting was wisdom. He knew in that moment he'd be okay. He'd trade giving up for letting go and the next rut he fell into he knew he wouldn't be there too long.

***

There's an old Buddhist saying, maybe it's Taoist, same difference: *everything is this, everything is that.* The story starts, there was a farmer. The farmer had a horse, and this farmer used his horse to work the fields. One day the farmer's horse ran away. The village people heard of the farmer's circumstance and unanimously agreed, "this is very unfortunate." The farmer responded, "is that so," and remained largely indifferent to the situation. He carried on with his work, farming longer hours to make up for the missing labour. After a week's time the farmer's horse returned, and with it five other wild horses. When the village people heard of the farmer's circumstance, they all agreed, "this is very providential." The farmer, as he had responded to the earlier consensus, said, "is that so," and did not permit his emotions to be swayed by the new, seemingly favourable, situation. This farmer had a son; a strong young man who also helped around the farm. When the new horses arrived the father employed his son to tame the wild beasts and prepare them for work in the field. While the son was working with the horses, one of them became freighted and bucked its hoof at the young man. The strike broke the son's leg. When the village people heard of the son's injury they hung their heads and all lamented, "this is a grave, grave, misfortune." The farmer, hearing this, did not agree, nor did he disagree, he simply stated, "is that so." A week following the injury, the majesty's army visited the town and conscripted all the able bodied young men to fight a territorial battle in a distant land. All the young men in the village were taken except the farmer's son.

Everything is this, everything is that.

Jeffrey stared at his phone. Every few minutes he'd pick it up, check the messages, then put it back down. There weren't any messages. There weren't any missed calls. Not that he would have responded if there were, he simply wanted to know that somewhere other than where he was, somebody was thinking of him. On the table beside his phone was the revolver his grandfather gave him before he passed. Before his grandfather *died.* Society has conditioned everyone to use softeners when it comes to death, but that detracts from its permanence. This revolver, Jeffrey had never shot it, but he was confident it would fire when he decided to pull the trigger. When he decided to *squeeze* the trigger. His grandfather had told him never to pull the trigger; *squeeze* it. "It should be a surprise," his grandfather had said. That was six years ago now. For six years this revolver had laid in a shoebox at the top of his closet. Six years his grandfather had laid in an oak box underground.

Worm food.

Jeffrey picked up his phone again, checked the spam folder of his text messages, and dialed his voicemail to see if a call had been misdirected there. Nothing. Outside his window he could see the neighbour's dog *frolicking* in the yard. Jeffrey used to hate that dog. It always barked at him. It was always shitting or pissing or barking. Today though, through the glass, in the sunlight, the dog looked like it was smiling. Its tongue flapped freely as it ran through the yard. He would dart from one tree to the next, bounce into the pile of leaves, pick up a new scent, and bolt toward the water's edge.

Jeffrey looked around his house. It looked like a bachelor lived there. It was a fitting look. Jeffrey *is* a bachelor. His wife had left. The girlfriend that followed left, too. This last relationship was the one that had him contemplating his exit. What a girl. She was great, Jeffrey thought. Except not at the end. Too many memories. That thing about how you think you own your memory but your memory owns you.

That.

Outside Jeffrey's window the dog was barking madly at a duck swimming by in the pond. Jeffrey didn't mind this barking, he even kind of liked it. The dog was barking and then finally jumped in the water to swim after the duck. Barking and swallowing gulps of water until finally the dog realized the more he barked the closer he would come to drowning. Instead, the dog swam with as much vigor, only without barking, but it was no use. Whenever the dog would get close the duck would flap its wings and fly just out of reach.

Finally, the dog gave up and made its way to shore. He shook the way only a dog can shake to rid himself of water. All the little droplets of wet glistened in the sunshine. Before the last drop disappeared into the air the dog was off again, charging toward some unknown object, tongue hanging free, a grin resting on his face as he ran.

Not a care in the world, Jeffrey thought.

Jeffrey looked at his phone, he looked at his grandfather's revolver, he looked at his lonely wedding band, and he started to laugh.

"What the fuck was I thinking?" he said out loud. "Over a girl? Jesus. Someone who wouldn't even cry at my funeral."

He picked up the revolver and emptied the bullets onto

the table. He picked up his phone and turned it off.

Outside Jeffrey's window he couldn't see the dog anymore. Jeffrey thought he was probably drawn into the field out of view, chasing something, or chasing nothing, simply being a dog and loving every minute of it. Dogs are content when they sit. They're happy when they're lying down. They're overjoyed to be running, or playing fetch, or wrestling. They're comfortable being dogs.

Jeffrey looked around his house. He looked at all his things. The TV he never turned on. The sectional. He looked at the kitchen table and the piano and the guitar and desk and the bookshelf and the closet filled with too many jackets and the shoe rack stacked with too many shoes and thought about his bedroom that had a wardrobe filled with too much clothes and the garage filled with even more things he never touched, or used only once. He thought about the dog and he laughed. He laughed like a crazy person. He laughed until tears streamed down the side of his cheeks. He laughed until his stomach hurt.

Jeffrey laughed because all of the *stuff* he had, everything he owned, he realized that he wasn't attached to any of it. All his life working jobs, working a career, trading his time for money, selling himself as a slave for what? To consume?

He looked around the house again. *The* house, no longer *his* house and thought about each item individually. He stood up from the table and walked into the kitchen, and his bedroom, and the bathroom. He walked out the front door and into the garage looking at everything in there. The car.

With each item he wondered if he'd be okay without it. If he'd miss it.

He started laughing again. There was nothing in his life,

pictures, or anything, that he'd be upset about losing. He thought about the relationships that had ended, he thought about his entire life and all his experiences, and then he thought about the dog. Jeffrey thought about the dog and he wondered what it would be like to *be* a dog. Not actually a dog, but *free*. That thing about the things you own and how they end up owning you.

That.

"This is crazy," Jeffrey said. He was thinking how someone can't just get up and go. What about their job or friends or family or *stuff*. "What about it?"

He thought why couldn't he just leave. Walk away from it all. Travel. See the world. Go where he wanted. The reality is, he was only living where he was because of his wife. Then stayed because of the girlfriend, and the one after her. This wasn't his *home*. He didn't have a home.

Walking back to the house, the neighbour dog jumped out from around the corner and startled Jeffrey. Instead of barking, as the dog usually did, he cocked his head to the side, grinned as only a dog can grin holding a glint of dare in his eyes, then bolted down the hill. Without a pause, Jeffrey chased after the dog.

Jeffrey ran down the hill as fast as he could, and like anyone who's ever ran down a hill as fast as they could can attest, Jeffrey got tripped up and tumbled into a roll near the bottom. The dog circled back and came within a couple feet of Jeffrey, panting. Jeffrey jumped to his feet and ran toward the water's edge. The dog chased after, and when within a couple feet, dodged around Jeffrey and took off in his own direction. Jeffrey pursued and this game continued for the rest of the afternoon. In the end, Jeffrey sat down on a rock near the water and the dog joined him.

Jeffrey petted the dog for quite some time, silently, both staring off in the distance. They must have been out there for hours, just sitting, because before Jeffrey realized it the sun was setting behind the trees. Jeffrey looked down at the sleeping neighbour dog and said, "Well Boy, thanks." The dog turned his head in acknowledgement and slowly began to rise.

They walked up the hill together. At the top, without saying a word, they separated, the dog to the neighbour house, Jeffrey to his.

Standing in the doorway Jeffrey took a deep breath and exhaled completely. On the table was the revolver he'd left. Beside the revolver was his phone, off. His wedding band lay between the two. "I'm going to do it," he said to himself.

Back outside, Jeffrey opened the garage and pulled the car into the driveway. He left it running, exited the vehicle, and grabbed the gas can from under the workbench. Jeffrey walked back to the house and into the dining room where earlier in the day he'd been sitting at the table. He scooped up the revolver, pocketed the bullets and went into the living room.

He poured gasoline on the sectional. He splashed gasoline on the walls.

In the dining room he poured gas on the table and on the phone and on the piano and over the guitar.

In the bedroom he soaked the bed and doused the wardrobe.

The bathroom was all tiles so he didn't pour anything in there, but in the kitchen he splashed whatever gasoline remained in the can.

Standing in the doorway, Jeffrey smiled. He pulled out a lighter and knelt to the floor. With one flick the floor was ablaze. The floor lit the island and the island the ceiling. The walls caught next and then the hall. Everything went up in flames. Everything Jeffrey had worked his entire life for. Everything that once seemed so important was now burning.

"I have lost nothing," Jeffrey said. "I have all my goods with me."

Leaving the door open, he walked casually toward the car and got in.

In the rear view mirror, Jeffrey could see the smoke billowing from the front door. As he drove away he removed the revolver from his front pocket and stashed it in the glove box. He wasn't going to be needing it. Jeffrey was free, at least for the moment, and there is no greater feeling known to man than freedom.

Even if it did taste like gasoline.

In the distance he could hear the wailing of a firetruck's siren as it tore down the back country roads from town toward what once was his house. If Jeffrey would have listened closer he might have heard the neighbour dog barking. Or he might not have, as in the silence the two of them shared that afternoon, the dog understood all that was about to happen, even if Jeffrey hadn't at the time.

Jeffrey was now free.

Everything he once loved was gone. Everything he once owned, burned. In his glovebox was the revolver his grandfather had gifted him, that one day if Jeffrey ever forgot his freedom he could load, insert into the back of his throat and squeeze the trigger.

One day.

Inspiration is a flash of lightning ripping from the ground into the ether leaving only a shadow where once a bright light assaulted the darkness. Lighting transforms; it obliterates. Lightning changes everything.

Growing up Terrance never wanted to be a painter. Not that he didn't *want* to be a painter only that he never *thought* to be one. He wanted to be a fireman. He wanted to be a police officer. A Fire Chief or Police Chief; both, just like his father. Terrance wanted to be James Bond. He wanted to be a professional athlete. Terrance wanted to be what every little boy wanted to be when they were growing up and still believed they could be anything they dreamed. With all the occupations in the world, being a painter didn't score high on the *cool*ness scale of things to aspire to. There's nothing particularly wrong with painting, only that growing up, being a painter didn't have that much appeal. Besides, thinking about the future, thinking about being a grown up, isn't being a painter kind of a strange profession for a grown man? No matter. Terrance never wanted to be a painter, so he never thought these things.

As he grew, as life turned, as life often does, Terrance forgot all the dreams about all the things he wanted to be when he was little and *settled* into a routine life. After high school he went to college. After college he got a job. Terrance married a girl he met in school and started a family. Two kids and two student loans later, Terrance and his wife did what most people do. They stopped living. They forgot what it was like to.

Their mornings began when their alarm clock rang. Not that their alarm clock rang anymore, Larissa had seen an ad on The View for an app that was supposed to wake them in their lightest sleep to a sound less intrusive than the buzz of an alarm clock. Their mornings now started with a recording of the ocean. There once was a time when waking up meant sex, but not anymore. Now sex was scheduled the way their kids swimming lessons were scheduled. And this was never a first thing in the morning event. This was a once a week appointment.

Waking up in the morning led to plugging in the coffee machine and making a pot of coffee. The coffee machine had an automatic brewing function that could be set the night before and be ready first thing in the morning; however, the hydro company had mailed out a public service bulletin informing homeowners that plugged-in appliances sucked energy like vampires sucked blood when they weren't in use. To stop these energy vampires and conserve electricity to ultimately lower their household energy bill, the bulletin advised homeowners to unplug whenever they could. Neither Terrance or Larissa had noticed a change in their electricity bill, though they continued the habit of unplugging and this meant brewing their own pot of coffee each morning.

They didn't mind the sacrifice.

While the coffee brewed, Larissa woke the kids and got them dressed for school. Terrance made them breakfast while he watched the news. Another school shooting. Another terrorist attack. Another celebrity checked into rehab. Another forgotten celebrity accused of sexually assaulting another nobody. Terrance always switched off the television when the kids came to the table figuring they didn't need to see any of the terrible things that were the preoccupations of adults everywhere. They would learn soon enough that the greatest days of their lives were behind them and would never be again.

After breakfast, Terrance would see the children off on the bus while Larissa showered and prepared to leave for work. Larissa always left first. Her career choice: a curator at the art museum. Terrance taught English Literature at the community college and only in the afternoons. Kissing her a passionless kiss goodbye, he closed the door behind and did what he always did once his wife and kids had left for the day. Terrance loaded the dishwasher and then cleaned himself up.

Mundane and lifeless was his reality.

At least until the day lightning struck.

On this particular morning, while loading the dishwasher, while feeling somewhat guilty about loading the dishwasher when it would be easy and more cost effective to wash them by hand, Terrance dropped one of the glasses his son had used during breakfast. The glass shattered when it struck the floor and shot shards of glass under the refrigerator. Glass exploded under the stove. Glass was strewn everywhere. Without getting angry, without any *real* emotion, Terrance went to the linen closet and retrieved the dustpan. Returning to the kitchen, he began sweeping up the glass, being sure to collect it all so neither Larissa or the kids would step on anything. As he swept, the smell of orange juice filled his nostrils and he remembered a time when he dreamed of owning an orchard of orange trees. He was swept into a vision of waking up to the actual sound and smell of the ocean; a summer breeze blowing through the window, the transparent white of the curtains dancing gently. He would smile waking without an alarm. He'd lean over and kiss his wife's forehead. He'd kiss her cheek and ear and neck and they'd make love. Terrance dreamed they'd wake up slow together and have fresh fruit for breakfast before heading out to the field to tend to the oranges. For lunch they'd eat something from their garden and nap in the hammock that overlooked the water. The afternoon would be him and his wife, swimming, laughing, and making love a second time before supper. The evenings were for drinking homemade wine and playing music under the stars. Laughing and loving and singing and dancing would be his life, always.

The stab from a piece of glass jolted Terrance from his daydream. Blood immediately began to flow from the cut on his knee. Terrance hadn't seen the shard on the floor as he swept. "Shit," he cursed aloud before dropping the dustpan and brush on the floor.

Terrance went to the washroom and retrieved the first aid kit and tweezers, then sat on the edge of the bathtub to examine the wound. The sting of the alcohol swab caused his face to crinkle but at least now he could see the glass lodged in his skin. Using the tweezers he pinched the shard and pulled it free. Blood oozed from the wound and Terrance wiped it away, wincing once more before applying a Band-Aid.

He washed his hands.

Then it happened.

The lightning.

A flash ripped through his mind and disappeared, leaving a shadow seared in its place.

Lightning transforms, remember. It obliterates.

Lightning changes everything.

In that moment, standing in front of the mirror, Terrance was inspired.

Leaving the mess on the kitchen floor, leaving the first aid kit abandoned in the bathroom, Terrance walked straight to

Larissa's art room and began rummaging through her supplies. He needed to paint. That's what inspiration is like. It grips. It commands. When inspiration comes, if it's not acted upon immediately, it disappears forever.

Terrance found the blank canvases and shuffled through the stack. At first he considered using a small canvas. Then he found it more appealing to work with a large one. As Terrance flipped through the stack of canvasses leaning against the wall, he eventually settled on one not too small or large, but something in between; a canvass just right.

He took Larissa's easel and left her art room. It was Larissa's art room after all and Terrance wouldn't have felt comfortable acting on his inspiration there. Terrance erected the easel in the family room in front of the patio doors. Outside, the sun was shining brightly over the lake, over the trees, and its warmth could be felt through the glass.

Terrance smiled.

As a child, Terrance never thought about being a painter. Now, in this moment, on this particular day, being a painter is all Terrance wanted to be. Facing the canvas, but looking out the window, Terrance thought about all of the great artists of antiquity. He thought of great writers. He thought of great musicians. Terrance wondered if when they made their masterpiece, they knew as he did, in that moment, that what they were about to create would be what they were remembered for.

He thought they must have.

Instead of returning to Larissa's art room for a paintbrush and paint, instead of going to his study for a pencil or a pen, Terrance went to bathroom and cleaned up his mess. He put away the rubbing alcohol. He returned the first aid kit and tweezers. Terrance washed out the sink. In the kitchen, Terrance picked up the dustpan and brushed the pieces of glass into the garbage. Then he returned the dustpan and brush to the linen closet, took out the vacuum, and vacuumed the kitchen making sure he'd collected everything.

With both messes cleaned and the dishwasher loaded, Terrance went to the bedroom to make the bed. Terrance always slept on the side closest to the door. In case of intruders he'd be the buffer between the assailant and his bride. He doesn't remember where he'd picked up this idea, but he knew he'd always slept closest to the door for this reason; hotels and everything.

Terrance went to his nightstand on his side of the bed and opened the drawer.

Under the notepad, under the Stephen King book, at the very bottom of the drawer was what the salesman had described as the gun with the right mix of durability, reliability, and shootability, *with the right price tag.* At the very bottom of his nightstand's drawer was a Glock handgun. Terrance picked it up. He didn't keep it loaded, in case the kids were ever snooping, however he did keep the magazine close at hand should one of those intruders venture in during the night. Terrance lifted the mattress and picked up the Glock's magazine. In one swift motion, like he'd practiced so many times before, he slipped the magazine into the handgrip of the gun and cocked the action.

He remembered the first time he held the gun in the store and recalled the power he felt standing there. Terrance noticed that holding the gun made him feel more than human.

He liked that feeling.

Terrance retuned to the family room and stood in front of

the easel. For the first time since he was a child, he felt alive. He didn't feel *settled*. Terrance wasn't following the script of routine; he was tearing it up. Terrance had a masterpiece to be painted, a masterpiece that needed to be painted, and it needed to be painted now.

Terrance knelt on the carpet in front of the easel and positioned the gun under his chin. The barrel pointed straight into where his brain was housed. He thought about putting the gun into his mouth and tried, but after a few seconds of attempting the right angle, he returned to his initial position. He bowed his head forward slightly and took his last breath.

The gun exploded as the glass of orange juice had earlier. The top of Terrance's head followed suit.

Blood splashed the canvas. Blood splashed on the walls. Blood splashed on the ceiling and on the patio doors. Pieces of grey matter, pieces of Terrance's brain stuck to the center of the canvas adding a texture that complimented the bits of skull.

Terrance's hand dropped the gun. His arm dropped. His body slumped.

The gun fell to the carpet.

Terrance fell to the carpet.

Blood soaked the carpet.

Blood painted the entire room.

On canvas the blood dripped slowly.

This was Terrance's masterpiece. His flash of inspiration. What he'd be remembered for. The dripping blood looked like dripping wine; legs in a wine glass. If Terrance could have seen his creation, he would have concluded: it is finished.

EVERYBODY ASKS FOR A SIGN

"A four inch tongue can bring a six foot man to his knees."

A few years ago the Word of Life Church of God in Christ bought a mobile sign board to divert the attention of drivers as they drove past the vacant church lot. Now it seemed as if every church in town had one. Before the signs had come to make you want to gouge out your eyes or van Gogh your ear they were cute like the way she chewed her food or how she called out "Hello," whenever she came home from work.

"Forgiveness is to swallow when you want to spit."

The signs used to say churchy things like "Honk if you love Jesus," but same as everybody copying the billboard exploit, when the Lutheran Church posted an explicit message, the rest of the herd followed suit. Nobody does anything original anymore. If you don't count the two Jehovah's Witness assembly halls, I pass twelve churches on my drive through town.

"The best gift a mother ever gave was time spent on her knees."

Last week the New Baptist Church's sign read, "A loose tongue gets into tight places," today it reads, "Sunday's Message: Jesus said, bring me that ass."

The rain has me constantly adjusting the speed of the wiper blades.

"God enters by a private door into every individual."

On the radio, the talk show host is asking callers to comment on the Supreme Court's decision to allow Niqāb's to be worn while taking the oath of citizenship. If you don't know what a Niqāb is, with a slit cut in a black pillowcase to see through, pull it over your head and look in the mirror. In what we use to arrest bank robbers for wearing and in fear of violating the right to Freedom of Religion this eastern fashion accessory has been adopted as an acceptable headdress to be worn while confirming identity.

A female caller complains how she was charged by the Liquor Board for selling booze to a 14-year-old boy wearing a Niqāb in Toronto.

"With God, size never matters."

Whether the rain has stopped or I've driven beyond the cloud, I no longer have to fiddle with the wiper toggle and leave it to rest. Despite the looks I might encourage I'm still going to wash my car when I get to town. Rain doesn't wash anything away, it only moves the dirt around.

"Bored? Try a missionary position."

"God's favourite word is come."

I smile passing the Catholic Church. With two lines they broadcast, "We love" and "hurting people." I don't think it reads the way they meant it to. This must be the church my wife attends. She's always saying things followed by "That's not how I meant it." I've started to think these slips are her passive aggressive way of getting a jab in. Today was the first time I walked out during one of her *discussions*. The therapist will tell me I was exhibiting maladaptive behavior. How when you're a kid and your parents tell you to ignore the taunts of a bully and just walk away, it was a good strategy then but as adults we're supposed to have learned to use our words.

"When you are in Him and He is in you, great things happen."

We've only been to counseling twice together but already it feels like fool me once shame on you, fool me twice shame on me. Talking with my friend Marty, he says, back in the good old days men could just leave, go out for a pack of cigarettes and never return. Leave the wife, leave the kids, leave the house. Start a new life somewhere else. There was nothing anybody could do about it. The wife would be left telling her friends, "I don't know what happened, he went out for a pack of cigarettes and never came back."

That was before GPS and the internet.

That was before alimony.

She'd probably go after some sort of payment on top of getting the house. Thank God we don't have kids; as irrelevant as *She* is.

"In your right hand are pleasures forever. Psalms 16:11."

Enough rain drops have accumulated that I have to turn the wipers back on.

"Open your mouth and I will fill it."

Seriously.

A PARDONABLE OFFENCE

People don't take responsibility for their actions anymore, so when someone does it's shocking. If the outcome here had been any other way it might have debuted on *To Catch a Predator*. People sitting in their living rooms after dinner, eyes fixed on the TV screen as Chris Hansen's voice narrated all the inappropriate things one twisted individual forced on another. Terrible stories of older men raping younger women. This story might have been one of them.

Outside your patio doors you can see the neighbour girl kicking a soccer ball in her back yard. You think to yourself how much she's grown since her family moved in just those few years ago. It was your birthday. After they finished unloading the moving van you went over to introduce yourself and welcome them to the area. Their daughter must have been nine years old at the time. Too shy to say 'hi,' she just looked up at you with those bright blue eyes peeking out from behind her father's leg before turning to run inside their new home. She reminded you of innocence. She reminded you of when you were a boy, too young to have learned the cruel lessons of life. Too young, period.

This neighbour girl, she's thirteen now. Three weeks ago she had her own birthday party slash end-of-the-school-year party. Over the years you've come to realize that her parents are the type of parents who will do anything for their little girl, and the type of parents who will let her do anything – as long as she does it at home so they can keep an eye out. The parties are always at their house; the barbeques, the sleepovers, everything always there. The only reason you know this last party was her thirteenth birthday party is because her and one of her little girlfriends knocked on your door and invited you to stop by. Obviously you didn't, because she's thirteen.

Since that first shy introduction, she and her little girlfriends have knocked on your door plenty of times. Asking permission to fish from your shoreline. Asking permission to snowboard on your hill in the winter. Asking you to buy her Girl Guide cookies. Asking you to sponsor her Jump Rope for Heart. To buy her cookie dough. You don't even bake the stuff but you buy it anyway because that's what good neighbours do.

Knocking on your door to collect bottles for her school's Bottle Drive.

Knocking on your door and running away giggling.

Out back she's kicking the soccer ball around and you can't help but notice how her tits have really come in. You notice how your once shy neighbour girl has really *developed*. Every once in a while as she skips through her yard with the soccer ball, she looks up toward where your deck is to make sure you take notice. She's the kind of girl who knows she's becoming a woman and wants people to take notice.

At night you see her peeking out her bedroom window down to where you're fishing. Her bedroom window overlooks your yard like your deck overlooks hers. That night when you catch her peeking through her bedroom window, ducking out of sight whenever you glance over your shoulder, that night, you've had a couple drinks.

You imagine what it would feel like to have her tiny little hands stroking your cock.

You know you shouldn't let your mind entertain these thoughts, but what the hell, you can't get in trouble for the things you think. Besides, it's not like you would ever act on it, it's just foolish wonderings.

The sun has set for the evening. In front of you, the still water of the lake reflects the moon's glow. Behind you, the light from your neighbour girl's bedroom creeps across the yard. She's left her blinds open and she's dressing into her pyjamas. You can see her silhouette in the window and you imagine running your hands over her newly teenage body. She clicks her light out and you realize you've had too much to drink.

The next day she knocks on your door and asks you for some newspapers so she can have a fire in the back yard. Schools out for summer and she and her girlfriend want to have one last bonfire before her family leaves for summer vacation. Her parents own a summer home in Vermont. Each summer, on the Saturday following the last day of school, your neighbours pack up and drive off only to return the last Friday before school begins again. You tell her to wait there and you'd bring the recycling in from the garage.

Returning to the kitchen, she's exactly where you left her, except she's taken off her clothes. Leaning against the front door, she's naked. She locks the deadbolt and tells you she wants you to take her. She says she's seen the way you look at her and that it was the way she's wanted you to look at her. She tells you that she's loved you since she was a little girl, since the very first moment you met. She tells you that all the girls in her class talk about their older lovers, and how she needs you to be the one to take her virginity.

All of this she tells you as she advances. Pressed up against your body, her hands cupped around the outside of your pants, you're throbbing. Her white skin taught smooth. She's perfect. Her tits have life in them, plump and perky, like you imagined. Looking up at you with those widened blue eyes she tells you if you don't, she's going to tell her parents you tried.

She says this smiling.

She says this like a girl who knows what she wants and always gets it.

She says it and begins to slink down to her knees. The curve of her hips rest against her naked legs. This neighbour girl moves slowly to undo your belt and unzip the fly of your jeans. She moves like she's waiting for permission, testing how far you'll let this go. Reaching her hand into your boxers, your neighbour girl, she grips your dick and you feel like exploding. You stand there frozen, expecting at any moment for a battalion of police officers to come crashing through the door like they do on TV, forcing you to the ground, smashing your face off the linoleum, your dick exposed, hard, and being bent under your body in excruciating pain. You imagine her bawling, telling them how you made her do it. How you told her if she didn't you would hurt her. Your neighbour girl thanking them for saving her before you made her do unspeakable things. Her parents running over to your house frantic and screaming. Her dad yelling how he's going to kill you. Her mom scooping up their little girl while threatening how you'll be treated in prison. Both parents yelling how your ass will be torn open because you're just like Ted Bundy. Constable 'I-eat-pieces-of-shit-like-you-for-breakfast,' advising you your right to remain silent. Reciting that everything you say can and will be used against you in a court of law. Spouting off all those lines you hear on TV as he slaps the cuffs on your wrists and smashes your face off the roof of his cruiser as he shoves you into the back seat, dick still hanging out, mashed and now bleeding.

All of this flashing in your mind as your neighbour girl continues to look up at you, hands full and her mouth resting on the tip of your penis. Her eyes begging for your consent.

"It will be our secret," she whispers.

You drop the newspapers on the counter and like any man with a gun to his head about to lose everything, you say, "fuck it," and carry her into your bedroom.

You tell yourself she doesn't look thirteen. Her breasts, her eyes. You convince yourself she's a woman; this neighbour girl, she came on to you. You thought she was older. Anything that you might use as a defence, knowing each to be about as strong as your self-control.

You don't even bother rationalizing anymore. She did it. It was her fault. At the very least it wasn't your fault, and then you press yourself into her pouting lips.

You can see she's in just a little bit of pain but she doesn't complain. Instead she moans a light moan; a moan like she's seen in the movies. She arches her back so that her stomach lifts off the bed. She presses the side of her head into the mattress.

Biting her bottom lip, your neighbour girl, she smiles.

You think about fucking her hard to teach her a lesson for this stunt she pulled. You think about fucking her to have her pain become digging her nails in your back, but you suddenly realize you're about to blow and barely have time to pull out.

A light flow of red trickles down her thigh.

At least that part of her story was true.

Falling on the bed beside her, she reaches her arm across your chest and asks you if she did okay. You assure her she did and kiss to the top of her head.

After a few minutes of lying on the bed, you clean her up and send her home with the newspapers she came for. As she leaves, she reaches up to kiss you on the cheek and whispers, "Our little secret."

That weekend her family is packing their Trailblazer and getting ready to leave.

You're thankful for this tradition of theirs because it will give you time to think about what happened. It will give you time to prepare a defence. Give time to wonder if it might happen again, if you would do it again, if you should do it again; how you could do it again. If you could get away with it and how far you could keep pushing the envelope. Taking that inch and making it a mile. Before your neighbours even leave their driveway, your fear of getting caught has been trumped: you're a man and you'll do whatever the fuck you want.

That whole summer you picture your neighbour girl coming home: her pleading eyes and sun-kissed skin. You imagine her sneaking over during the day, at night, whenever her parents aren't home. Your mouth waters at the thought of how clean she tasted. You throb at the thought of her.

The week before her family should have returned home you get a letter in the mail. The handwriting on the envelope is gentle, the kind of rounded letters that make you happy to read. You guess it's from her and open it.

The letter is addressed: My first and only.

In this letter she tells you how all summer she hasn't stopped thinking about your one time together; how she never told anyone and wasn't going to.

She writes how even though you probably didn't believe her when she said it, she loves you.

She tells you about all the fun things she and her parents have been doing in Vermont: the nights under the stars, the days at the beach, their shopping trips into town. She tells you about all the things a thirteen year old girl would write to her boyfriend.

As casually as she recollected her summer vacation she tells you how she missed her period. How one day in town, when her parents weren't around, she bought a pregnancy test. She wrote how her parents would kill her if they ever found out and how they'd kill you, or worse.

She loves you and so she could never let this happen. She meant it when she said, "our little secret."

In this letter she tells you that she's going to kill herself before they return home.

Teenage girls are insufferably dramatic.

She described it as a romantic tragedy, a very real Romeo and Juliet, and signed the letter, "Always, our little secret."

The following week, when your neighbours were supposed to return home, they didn't. It's not until sometime in September they do and it's then you hear that their daughter is dead. That she killed herself. How she didn't leave a note.

Your neighbours are devastated.

You hear about how she did it.

You assumed it was swallowing a handful of pills, but you assumed wrong. Your neighbour girl went out hard. She was strong. She gave herself no way of retreat.

If you want to take the island you have to burn the ships.

Your neighbour girl, what she did was, she drew a bath. At their summer home, off her parent's bedroom was an oversized bathroom with one of those old claw foot tubs in the center. Three sides of the room are lit up by the sun that shines through the white framed windows. The view is the lake.

Your neighbour girl, she drew a hot bath. As the tub filled, she opened the medicine cabinet of her parent's bathroom and swallowed two Aspirins. She took out her daddy's shave kit. He's one of those types of men who wet shaves with a badger brush and straight razor. She removed one of the wax wrapped doubled edged blades from inside the kit and set it on the ledge of the bathtub before undressing. With the tub full she shut off the water then folded her clothes into a pile on the chair.

Bath drawn, Aspirin popped, and razor blade resting on the ledge of the bathtub, she eased her naked body into the water. Her white skin turned pink from the heat as she allowed herself to soak. A Mona Lisa smile on her face as she looked out the windows to a world whose condemnation for love is death.

Soaking in the hot bath, your neighbour girl picked up the razor blade and ran it down the length of her arm. If it was a cry for help she would have scratched across her wrist. The razor blade split the skin with ease and opened her veins just as effortlessly. Wrist to elbow, one straight line, your neighbour girl, she was something fierce.

With the Aspirin thinning her blood and the water warming her body, blood poured from her arm like it was waiting for its moment to escape.

As she started on the other arm, she passed out. Lying there, slumped in the hot bath in the claw footed tub, her parents returned from town. They found her soaking in their bathtub, hair hanging over the ledge, and the merlot water steaming the sweet copper scent of lifeless beauty.

They didn't know about her being pregnant.

They didn't know anything.

Your neighbour girl, at least she did the right thing.

THERAPY

If I have to hear about one more bullshit reality TV show during dinner again I'm going to take my fork and start stabbing her in her stupid blue eyes. No joke, this goes for anyone. I come with a disclaimer now: mention what MacRoy said on Big Brother or how Kaitlyn took two guys into her private suite on the Bachelorette and I'll use whatever means available to crush your fucking skull. Don't test me. I don't even own a TV and I still have to hear about those twats on Duck Dynasty and 19 and Counting; Amazing goddamn Race. Just don't. Please.

Maybe that wasn't the best way to get started. That quip about how you never get a second chance at making a first impression. Well it's out there now and there's no taking it back. I'm really not a terrible person or anything. I just think that this recent obsession with Reality TV is soul deadening. Not that I believe we have a soul, but you know what I mean, right? Shit. This isn't getting any better. Can we start over?

I guess I'm here because, well, I think I'm depressed. I'm sure you hear that a lot. I don't mean I'm a whiner or some other pussy. Not that I think being in touch with your emotions is an effeminate trait. It's just an expression.

Well, I guess my dad used to tell me to 'man up' all the time, but this isn't about him. I don't buy into all that Fraud shit. I mean Freud; that was a slip. Let me rephrase. I don't think I'm depressed like other people think they're depressed. Well, I'm sure they're depressed because of *whatever*, but my depression is different. I think I might even enjoy it. That Smashing Pumpkins song, how does it go, in love with my sadness? How come you're not writing anything down? Do you have a recording device in here? This isn't what I expected at all.

I guess I thought well, first, you'd be a guy. I don't know why I thought that, I just pictured you as an older guy with glasses. You know, with one of those yellow notepads, me lying on my back on a leather couch, my hand slowly drifting toward my jeans then stroking my cock as you uncovered some secret desire I have to fuck dudes or something.

No, I'm not a homosexual. That was a joke. I started today talking about being on a date with a girl and her babbling on about reality TV, remember? Maybe you should be taking notes. Yeah, I am a little uncomfortable. I've never done this before. Can I shut my eyes and talk that way instead? It might help me focus.

If I'm being completely honest, I'm pretty sure my brain should be Swiss cheese, all the drugs I've done. My liver should be rot from all the drinking or at the very least my dick should be diseased. But nothing. Like I should be dead many times over but I'm not and this depresses the hell out of me.

No I don't do drugs anymore, why is that always the first question? I don't think there's anything wrong with doing drugs, I just can't bring myself to do them. That sounds cowardice, like I would, it's just right now I can't justify the expense or take the risk of winding up dead in a ditch, my brain fried from snorting Drain-O laced blow. My mom would be devastated and the thought of her tears kills me.

Yeah, we're pretty close. Last time I did drugs? That depends. To the world it was in high school, cocaine, once at a party; but this is between us, right? Then the last time actually was at Christmas with a girl I was dating. We picked up a couple grams and snorted the bag on Christmas Day.

No, it's not a problem. Everybody needs a little escape from sobriety now and again.

Drinking? Of course I drink. Nothing excessive, maybe a bottle of wine at night. Yeah, to myself. At home. That's actually why I decided to come in to see you in the first place.

No, not for a drinking problem, I don't have a drinking problem. It's not like I'm out driving drunk, playing bumper cars with all the ones parked on the side of the road or running over people like I was playing Grand Theft Auto. Just enough drink to take the edge off and fall asleep.

When it happened it was like that tipping point Malcolm Gladwell talks about. You know how everything in life compounds and stacks and balances and kind of sits there at an angle of repose, looking like it should come crashing down, but it doesn't? That. I actually saw a rock balanced like this once while I was at the Grand Canyon. When I was visiting Arizona I was determined to see the Grand Canyon so one day I rented a convertible and drove to the North Rim. The first few exits were packed with tourists so I kept driving. I don't really like crowds of people. It was a gamble but it turned out there was this fourth parking lot where there didn't seem to be too many visitors so I pulled in, got out, and walked toward where the canyon would be. It was incredible. I know its cliché, but the view is breathtaking, really, especially if you're afraid of heights. At this access they didn't even have barriers along the edge. It would have been so easy to push someone over. It would have been easy to jump. That's how fucking awesome this place was.

What? No, I'm not a psychopath. I was describing how liberated this place was, how uncontrolled it was by modern regulation. That's why they cover overpasses and put fences on the roofs of buildings, right? Suicide? So people don't jump to their death? Jumping's such a stupid way to kill yourself. There's too many variables. The height you have to be at, you're body weight, the surface material. There are just so many factors that could screw up the attempt. I've put a lot of thought into suicide and jumping is definitely not how I would stage my exit. What was I talking about?

Right. The angle of repose. The rock.

So I was walking along the path at the Canyon, and because there are no railings, you can get even closer if you leave the trail. Obviously I ventured off, just past the shrubs and onto the loose rock. That's when I saw it: this giant rock balancing above the drop. I don't know how to estimate rock weights, they're not chicks, but it was massive. Maybe twenty tons? Probably more; regardless, it just stood there, perfectly balanced, looking like the next gust of wind would blow it over but it never happened. I wondered how long it stood there like that or how come nobody ever ran out and tried to push it off. I thought about doing it myself, but damn, if I slipped it would be me over the edge instead of the rock and you know how I feel about suicide by jumping; though I'm sure at that height and my weight, a success would have been uncontested by the gods. Besides, I had to return the car that night and if I got hurt or arrested I didn't want to be stuck with another day's rental fees.

That's how it felt, though; like everything in my life had been balancing at a critical mass for so long and instead of staying balanced, it all came crashing down. I'm washing dishes the other morning, well it was actually after lunch. I slept in that morning. I don't know why I said morning. I've been doing that a lot lately.

Not mixing up morning and afternoon, I'm not retarded; lying. Not purposely either, it just comes out and I catch myself doing it and I'm like, 'Why did I just lie?'

You look confused. I'll explain.

So I'm very confident. Some people might call it arrogance but that's just because they're lacking confidence in themselves, which is pathetic. I know what I know and I don't waste time speculating on the things I don't. I'm fortunate to be this good. I don't pretend it has anything to do with me though, I can't take credit for being born where I was born, when I was born, with the genes I have; but I'm not going to be ashamed of my good fortune either. Gifts are only good if you use them a lot, right? Recently, when somebody asks me a question, I've found myself in the habit of responding with, 'I think…' when in actuality I know, not think. I've been playing down to other people's levels just so that they won't feel uncomfortable, and that doesn't benefit anyone.

It's not arrogance. Like I said, I don't speculate on the things I don't know, so when I say something I can say it matter-of-factly. I can't think of another example right now, but when people make inaccurate claims I don't even correct them and that's lying too. All those direct sales people peddling their miracle elixirs or the religious peddling their imaginary friends, I could correct them so easily but most times I just listen patiently in silence. I'm living in this tension between being authentic and trying to get along in the world and it's a terrible position to be in. I read this book recently called *Lying* by Sam Harris and he asked how our lives would be different if we decided not to lie anymore. It's a pretty simple concept but just because it's simple doesn't make it easy. In his book he asked, "what relationships would cease to exist because we would find that they could no longer be honestly maintained?" My mind detonated. I started noticing how often I lie for no reason at all and decided to take the challenge to not lie anymore. It's a pretty brazen concept. I don't make book recommendations very often because I hate when people recommend books to me, but this is one you should definitely check out.

At this rate we're never going to get to what brought me in to see you.

Okay, I was washing the dishes after lunch and the way I wash them, because there's only one sink, I pile all the utensils to the right of the drain plug while I'm filling it. I stack the pots and pans on the counter on the right of the sink with the cups lined up in front of them, then the plates and the bowls in behind. Everything's on the right because the drying rack is on the counter to the left. It just makes sense that way. I'm not going to wash the glasses or the plates after I've washed the greasy pans because it takes more effort to clean the film of grease off the other dishes, so I wash the pans last. I place the cups in between the plates and pans so they don't get bumped off the counter and break on the floor. I wash the plates first because they stack neatly at the back of the drying rack. It's all about logic. I've had girls over who wash the dishes all haphazardly, obviously having never given any thought to streamlining the process. It's embarrassing to watch. It's even dangerous if they stack them in the drying rack wrong.

You can stack dishes wrong. Everything's relative. You would never build a house by starting with the shingles. You start with the foundation. If you stack the glasses on top of the plates and pans and then make one wrong move, the glasses come crashing down. Anyway. I can't imagine seeing the way you stack dishes if your face is like that.

As the sinks filling I start to wash the plates and bowls before moving on to the cups and glasses. Reaching for my

91

coffee mug to wash, I guess I bumped the wine glass off the ledge. There I go again, 'I guess,' I don't guess, *I did;* see how bad it's gotten? I reached for my coffee mug and I bumped the wine glass off the ledge. I watched it happen too. That last red wine glass slip over the edge of the counter and fall the way lasts of anything fall in slow motion before smashing on the hardwood floor below.

I have no idea why the kitchen floor is hardwood, it was like that when I bought the place. I thought they were usually tiled or at the least linoleum.

Pieces of stem exploded across the floor. Shards of glass shattered. Soap bubbles and wet were mixed in the mess. I even said, "For fucks sake, man," out loud; and I was there all by myself. That's when my balancing rock came crashing down. That's how I knew I had to talk to someone. When you start speaking to yourself out loud, trouble is just around the corner. I mean there's always been a conversation in my head, that talking back and forth between resident devil and angel, but I've never given it a voice. Actually, mine's no devil and angel, it's more like a super computer calculating and evaluating everything. Am I walking too fast? How's my posture? How do people see me right now? How do I sound? Should I be smiling? What do they hear? Should I be using more eye contact or less eye contact? Too much eye contact might intimidate them; not enough may give the appearance I don't care. Should I cross my legs or lean forward with my elbows on my knees? Nonstop; all the time. As if I'm living on two planes of reality for everything.

The broken glass? No, I didn't clean up the mess. Well eventually I did, but not right away. I used to be OCD but I had to give that up. It was exhausting. What was it that

Nietzsche said, "know thyself and master your abilities?" I adopted the practice of constant never ending improvement and got over my annoying obsessions. That's why I have no patience for lethargic individuals. It takes very little effort to make tiny adjustments every day. You do this and before you know it you're exponentially different; improved. It's compounding interest.

You've never heard of compounding interest? Jesus. I thought you had to have a degree to do this kind of work?

Compounding interest is interest on interest, instead of interest simply on the principal amount. And if there's regular compounding periods, the returns are going to be huge in no time at all. If you're only yearly payments, then the returns will never reach what could have been if you condensed to daily compounding. A little bit each day, building on the day before and the day before that is how you become a god. Have you ever heard of the fifth dimension? Actually, you know what, let's not go down that rabbit hole. I don't know much about it and I'm not going to start talking out of my ass. Let's get back.

I finished the dishes first and then cleaned up the mess, vacuumed and all that. My last red wine glass though. It pretty near devastated me. After I put everything away I went into the living room and sat in my chair. It's this wooden legged red leather beast I have in the corner. At the end of every day I turn on the lamp and sit in my chair and drink my wine. It's probably the only thing I look forward to anymore. The end of the day, sitting in my chair under the soft yellow glow of the lamp with a bottle of red wine and drinking in silence. No chatter, no movement, no nothing except maybe the flicker of the bulb. The other night it was wine from Argentina, not that I know anything about wine, I just know it was from Argentina because it was beside the bottle of red from California that I usually buy. The label on the Argentina bottle commanded my attention so I chose it instead. I'd never seen the label before. In the center of the black background was a gold mask ablaze with thick peacock feathers. No year, no words, just this image. I asked the lady at the cash if she'd ever tried it. She hadn't even seen the bottle before. Naturally I bought it and when I brought it home I even *tasted* the wine before pouring myself a glass. I would have looked like such a fool if anybody was watching me, tasting the wine the way a server at a restaurant invites you to do before pouring a full glass, only alone. I opened the bottle and poured a splash into the glass. I let it sit briefly before giving it a swirl to allow the aroma to lift. I sniffed above the glass; strangers in restaurants stick their noses into the glass and that's when you know they have no idea what they're doing. It's nose above the glass and short quick sniffs. Then I tasted it. I even laughed at the absurdity of my theatrics; but it was fun. If you're not having fun, what's the point?

I poured a glass and drank, the whole time staring at the label. That label really got to me. The gold. The mask. I started getting all Socratic reflecting on how the unexamined life is not worth living and all that. I wondered how long I've lived with my own mask on, everybody wearing their own mask. It was deep. It was depressing. I must have spent half the night sitting and staring and thinking. In the end I was sufficiently drunk and went to bed. When the glass broke the next day I kind of entered into a trance because I remembered drinking the wine the night before and all the reflecting I was doing. I've been in a fog ever since.

When it happened, I retreated to my chair almost

mechanically and sat there staring at nothing. Thinking. The futility of life. The lack of meaning. The waste. As I spiraled down this train of thought, I expected to feel sad and burdened but as I contemplated each idea the exact opposite occurred.

The futility of life: a little less weight.

Life's meaninglessness: even lighter.

The waste: I'm nearly floating.

The realization that nothing matters was the most freeing idea I've ever had.

Zero! That's what it's called; that song by Smashing Pumpkins. What a great song. The first time I heard it was at a friend's house in grade school. I don't know if he was a real friend, I mean we're not friends anymore, but in grade school we hung out a lot.

Of course this has to do with what we were just talking about. It has absolutely everything to do with it.

This friend and I, we used to play all sorts of army games, even go on missions to shoplift from the toy store beside his house. We would plan it all out in detail with drawings and walkie-talkies and code names. We'd try to act all inconspicuous. We'd employ diversions. It's not like our petty shoplifting hurt anyone. Even at that early age we knew those corporations had tons of money and rationalized they weren't going to miss a few science kits and remote control cars. We'd take our plunder from a successful mission and mix up the chemicals and assemble little bombs. Kid stuff before iPads and Apps entered the scene. You should have seen some of the things we made. It was impressive. Even a few of the older kids thought so. I remember this one time we were prepping the walkie-talkies preparing for a mission we'd devised and my friend's older brother came up with an idea to re-enact a scene from Mission Impossible. It was the scene where Tom Cruise is aussie-repelling from a helicopter, falling face first toward the ground at a hundred miles an hour and at the last second pulls the cord to stop inches above splatter. Reflecting on it now, I think this older brother of his was a little sadistic. I wanted to be Tom Cruise so he tied the bungee cord around me. It was a long bungee cord and the balcony we were going to perform this stunt from was above about forty steps. All rigged up, we did a couple of practice runs before his older brother threw me off the ledge above the stairs. It was fun for about a second. That's how long it took for the cord to snap. I hit the ground hard and just lay there stunned like a stupid little kid. Everybody was freaking out thinking I was paralyzed. I wasn't, but all that attention was nice so I played it up. My friend's parents, they owned the Chinese restaurant in town, so they were old world type parents. I'm pretty sure they beat the shit of the brother. I wasn't hurt or anything, just startled, and learning quickly that play acting is better than real life. They even gave me ice cream afterwards and we never got ice cream in that house. There's always the chance that they just might have been trying to purchase my silence. It's funny how a song can bring you back to the place you first heard it. I haven't heard that song in forever, I don't even listen to music very often anymore. I got hooked on this 'Automobile University' racket and can't get enough of it. The theory is we spend so much time driving you can literally listen to years' worth of university lectures between destinations. You can download entire courses from Berkley or MIT and listen to them. You don't get the credit for it but I'm not after the piece of paper. I just want to know. I've always been autodidact. So now whenever I drive I make sure I have something educational playing in the CD player. It's doing this that I've had most of my psychological breakthroughs. I was listening to John Searle's course on the Philosophy of Mind and by the end of the lecture I'd lost my soul. That's how I describe the day I discarded the concept of being body and spirit. I was listening to this course in my car, driving an hour back and forth to work. I was a janitor at the time so an hour each way is quite far for menial work, but I didn't mind the alone time. I find being alone refreshes me. Either way, while I was driving I was listening to this lecture about Descartes and duality and how he popularized the soul and body idea. The professor explained how everything still makes sense without positing the idea of a soul; you'll have to listen to the lecture, but it was a life changing moment. I was like: holy shit; then my car began swerving. It was winter so I thought I hit a patch of black ice, but the car kept swerving sporadically and I noticed the other drivers in my rear view mirror starting to back off. I took the next exit and pulled onto the gravel shoulder. My rear tire had blown. I'd just put my winter tires on a few days before so I was really bummed out. To my surprise, a car stopped to help almost immediately. It was this little old lady. I didn't know what to expect. She got out of her car and approached me. "I can't offer you any help, but I just wanted to make sure you were okay." How often does that happen? This sweet old lady worried about my wellbeing. I don't know if it was her selflessness or the losing my soul a few moments before, but I gave her the biggest bear hug. I even lifted her off the ground in my excitement. She struggled free and hurried back to her car, but man, what a gesture. I call that day Liberation Day.

Do you mind if we switch seats? I like being able to see outside. When I'm at home, sitting at the table, I always sit in the chair where I can see out the patio doors. Sunny days, rainy days, even if it's night time and all I can see is the moon I always sit in the chair that lets me look outside.

I just like it.

You think it's some kind of metaphor for my life? Stuck inside always looking out to a world I wish I was part of? I know you didn't say that, but I've obviously thought it. I think it's a pretty generalized metaphor and if you're insinuating I'm gay again I won't tolerate it.

I'm not being hostile, just don't give me textbook responses. You get what you tolerate and I won't tolerate regurgitated insights. I won't fit into a textbook analysis. I'm different.

Sure, an outlier. I know how rare that is. I know everybody thinks they're special. I don't think that I'm special, I'm just different and so I expect to be treated that way. You know how everybody thinks they're a great driver? With all those idiots out there on the roads, everybody can't be a great driver; I am. There's nothing that pisses me off more than an inconsistent driver on the road. If you drive slow that's okay, just be consistent about it. Don't speed up when the road turns to a double lane and make it difficult for me to pass you and then slow down again when the passing lane ends. That's a dick move. Or how about someone riding your ass and refusing to pass. I think that pisses me off even more. If I was a road-tester, those people who issue driver's licences, I would fail ninety percent of the candidates that came through the door. I'm thankful I don't keep a gun in my car. When a driver really pisses me off I wish I could shoot them right in the face as I passed; seriously. Sometimes when I finally find the opportunity to pass a driver that's caused me all this frustration

I point my hand at them like it's a gun and press my thumb down like I'm blowing their head off.

I don't think that's extreme. They should know how their behavior makes me feel. Pretty much everything I do is above average so I have no tolerance for less than average. Maybe that's part of what depresses me, too, Doc: being so much better than most for so long. Always being better but never being passionate about anything.

The gun thing? You're not going to report that are you? I'm not planning on killing anybody, it was hyperbole. I don't even own a gun. I was exaggerating to emphasize how irritating I find inconsistency. I'm not a violent person. I've never even been in a real fight. Sure I've been punched in the face a few times but never a fight where there's a group of people standing around cheering. A fight where somebody is getting jerseyed and kneed to face over and over again; or a fight where people have to jump in to stop it because someone's going to die if they don't; blood everywhere. Never once, just guys being guys wrestling around.

I don't know why. I never saw the point in fighting. What does it accomplish? Have a fight and then spend the rest of your life having to look over your shoulder, always watching your back in case you bump into that person again. Why live with that fear?

Killing on the other hand I've thought about. I wouldn't do it, and I never think about it on purpose, I just find myself standing there in the moment, tumbling down a homicidal rabbit hole, before snapping out of it and laughing at the absurdity of it all.

You've never heard of tumbling? I guess you wouldn't have. It's the name I coined for murder fantasies.

The first time this happened to me would have been about fifteen years ago. I was at my girlfriend's aunt's cottage in the Muskoka's. It's such a beautiful area there. Her aunt and uncle owned a cottage in the woods that overlooked a private lake. They had a hot tub on their deck with different coloured LED lights in the lining that would change while you were soaking in it. My girlfriend's aunt was a teacher and her uncle was a Wall Street type. They each lived in their own house, her aunt at the cottage in Muskoka, her uncle in Toronto. They only saw each other on weekends. If I ever get married, I'd want an arrangement like that. I think having your own space is conducive to a lasting relationship. Anyway, my girlfriend and I would go up to this cottage every year and drink wine and hike and swim and all that. We'd have sex when her aunt was out running errands. Whenever her uncle came up on the weekends and he knew we were there he would bring a bottle of scotch for me and him to drink out in the garage. We would sit out there with the wood stove burning, drinking scotch and talking. Come to think of it, he might have been a little depressed, too. He'd tell me about the trades he made during week that hit big. He taught me how to spot the winners like he had learned to do when he was a younger man. After a few drinks he'd take the tarp off his Shelby, or whatever the car was he was building, and show me the engine. I don't know much about cars but it was nice to hear someone who was passionate about something talk about it. He kept fireworks in the cupboards above his workbench and when I found this out I showed him how to deconstruct them to make bombs. He loved it, so we blew a lot of shit up. This one night we were sitting there drinking scotch, talking, and it happened. I started tumbling.

I've noticed that when I start tumbling, the trigger is always the conversation. With the other person talking and talking and talking I sort of zone out. Then it's noticing a weapon nearby. Next, I just grab whatever the weapon is and use it to absolutely desecrate the person talking.

The axe in the corner had a wooden handle. The red head was chipped away so the brushed metal was exposed. I'm sitting in the garage drinking scotch, tumbling for the first time and you can imagine how hard it was for me. As he's turned to pour the next round of drinks I grab the axe. I lift it above my head and swing it down hard on his back. It got stuck in his shoulder. He kind of crumbled and I used my foot against his back to pull the axe free. He turned around in shock and looked at me like "What the fuck," so I took another swipe, this time at his head, and split his face. His stupid stunned face stared up at me frozen in time. It was horrible; but I kept chopping, clumps of his hair were getting stuck to the workbench. Chunks of his brain were being flung on each backswing. Blood was everywhere. The weirdest thing was how easy it was to do, so instead of freaking out I kept tumbling. I thought about cleaning up the mess, which would have been impossible, so I started thinking about killing my girlfriend and her aunt who were still inside the cottage. My girlfriend would probably come out with a snack at some point, or at least come out to tell us to wrap it up, so I decided that's when I'd get her. I'd hide behind the door to give her the chance to be shocked silent by her uncle's mangled body. Before she screamed I could have a chain around her neck choking her out while I forced her to the ground until she lost consciousness. The whole time I'd be squeezing tighter, sitting on top of her, and thumbing one of her eyes so she'd keep them closed. She had gorgeous eyes. Deep like the ocean. An azul. But then what? Go inside and kill her aunt? What if she heard the struggle and had a gun aimed at the door. Or worse, she'd seen all the excitement and called the cops. I'd be done for, forced to go on a killing spree. And to what end? That's the question. Fuck to be or not to be, I heard that guy was a plagiarizer, the question is always: to what end? And that's when I snapped out of it. When the tumbling starts to get a little bit crazy I snap out of it with a chuckle. Uncle Pete was looking at me all queer like, handing me the scotch, "You okay, kid?"

That was the first time.

Now when it happens people don't even notice I've tranced out. It was just that first time that caught me off guard.

This is confidential, right? I signed those papers last week? It's not like I'm planning a murder and making you an accessory or anything, these are just things that pop into my head. I'm sure everybody has them at least sometimes. They happen so regularly to me now I just assumed they're normal that people just supress them. Or is it repress? No matter. That first time shook me up but now I kind of look forward to them. They make the day interesting wondering when the next one will show up, how it will go.

Just the other day I was having dinner with a girl and afterwards we sat at the island in her kitchen drinking wine and talking. She was talking. How unique is that? Get a few drinks into her and she suddenly becomes an open book. A real Chatty Kathy. She's blabbering away about nothing and then the knife block on the counter catches my attention. It was a beautiful blackened wood knife block. Steel knives with gunmetal handles. They were truly a work of art.

Tumble away.

I remember thinking how easy it would have been to pull that chef's knife out and press it through the back of her shoulder blade. She wouldn't even have noticed me get up to do it, all her talking, and those sharp blades, the knife would have just slipped right in. Before she had the chance to scream I jabbed the knife into her throat, over and over again, holding her head back being careful not to cut myself. She reached up to grip her neck, they always do despite the uselessness of the gesture, so I spun her around and starting hacking wildly into her chest until she died. But then I had to worry about who knew I was there. If she told any of her friends about us, etcetera, etcetera, etcetera. If you're going to hack someone up, you'd better make sure no one can tie you to it.

That was the end of the tumble.

She remained completely unaware of what just happened, still blabbering on about her aspirations or something stupid. The good thing about those chatty ones though, they're usually great at giving head.

You look concerned. I'm not a psychopath. It's not like I choose to think these thoughts, they just pop into my head. Haven't you ever been to a meditation class? You're trying to sit still on your cushion and not think of anything, but no matter how hard you try, in spite of all your effort, things distract your attention. You get an itch. You need to shift. You think about your grocery list. What's for dinner? You think about your work. The thoughts endlessly appear. You're always told, "Like clouds in the sky, watch your thoughts float by, enjoy the show, nothing more to know; remain an amused witness of it all." That's what tumbling is like. I don't agree with much of what those quack gurus spout out, but when it comes to this I have to concede. They're like clouds in the sky, showing up whenever they want, so I let them float by and that's it. An amused witness.

I mean I ignore them mostly.

I shouldn't have even told you. I only did because I figured I wouldn't hold anything back. I'd give you everything I can to make your job easier. I thought that was the best approach. Let's just talk about something else. I'm starting to feel like an idiot. I really hoped being here would be different. I can never tell anybody what I'm actually thinking because they look at me concerned, like they're fucking scared.

I don't have anger issues, it's just, can you imagine going through your whole life feeling completely alone, like nobody in the whole world knows what you're feeling, what it's like to be you? All you'd want is one genuine connection, with anybody. Even if you had to pay for it, having one person get you.

I don't even know. That's what I'm trying to do, I want you to know what it's like, but if I can't tell you how I'm actually feeling how are we ever supposed to build that connection? How will you ever know? If I have to lie to you in here then what's the difference between all those other relationships I have out there? You know? Maybe that's enough for today. I'm not feeling a hundred percent anyway.

I'm not running away from my problems, this just isn't getting anywhere. Why do I have to do all the talking? I never even wanted to talk about this stuff. We kind of just stumbled on it. How about I tell you about my dream from last night? How about that? That will calm me down. It was weird, but it had this super erotic undertone. I haven't been able to stop thinking about it.

I was in the mattress section of a department store. I

don't know which store, they didn't wear uniforms or nametags, but it was a department store like Sears. I was trying out different mattresses and the saleswoman asked me how I slept at night. My mind went immediately to fucking, but you can't just come out and say how you want to sleep with every girl you see, so I answered her question in a leading way. I told her that it depends on whether I'm by myself or if someone is in bed with me. By myself I sleep on my back, with someone there I sleep on my side. She told me to show her, so I had her lay on the bed on her side and I spooned up next to her. I put my arm around her body and rested my hand gently on her breasts. I pressed the front of my pants against her ass. You know a girl is into it when she presses back a little, which she did, so I slowly started kissing her neck. I started nibbling her earlobes. All this right there on the mattress in the middle of the store. She loved it. We were moving in unison, dry humping and kissing. With our lips locked I traced my hands down her body and undid the button on her pants to slide them down her legs. Kissing her body I made it down to her panties and began sliding them off too. I love eating pussy. I'd only pulled them down a few inches when it was as if I got punched in the face by one of those spring-loaded boxing gloves. Right in the face. Layers of thick flower petals bloomed from this girl's cunt, but it wasn't flower petals, it was skin. I'd never seen anything like it. No bush whatsoever, she was cleanly shaven. And the lips weren't repulsive looking like a fat broads pancaked flaps; these lips were art. There was something delicate about the way her skin was layered leading back to her vagina. She lifted her head slightly and looked down at me looking down at her and smiled. She started biting on her bottom lip which aroused the hell out of me so I began licking furiously between each one of the petals. It was delicious. You know how some girl's pussies are just a dream to eat? Hers was. Each flap tasted like morning dew on a leaf. I would have stayed down there all day if my alarm didn't steal me away. I'll tell you one thing. Before I came here today, I stopped by The Brick to order a new mattress. I don't even believe dreams have any special meanings, but could you imagine?

My tastes are simple: books, wine, and women. I remember this one time at the rippers I was having a few drinks. I wasn't sitting in perverts row or anything, but I had a little table to myself near the stage. Girls kept stopping by intermittently trying to take me for a private dance. They'd tell me their daddy stories or how they were paying their way through college, but I learned young that these girls are like seagulls at the beach: you feed one of them and thousands come out of the woodwork poking around for scraps. Fucking strippers. I just wanted to enjoy a few pints and be left alone. All of these interruptions irritated me. After a few drinks I went to the bathroom to take a leak. This club had unisex bathrooms and when I opened the door there's this black stripper standing in front of the mirror with one leg up on the counter. She's hunched over her twat inspecting, using her fingers to move her lips around. Normal pussy lips. I thought she was looking for scabs or lice. Black girls usually keep a little bush down there so I imagine it's easier for them to catch a case of the critters. She must have noticed my stare and explained that she was looking for pieces of toilet paper. Apparently, on stage, toilet paper shows up quite bright on a black girl's pussy because of the black lights or something.

This turned my night right around. I still laugh thinking

about it. I never would have thought that in a thousand years.

Yeah, I'm currently single. Why would you ask that? It's not because I can't get a girl, I can get a girl. I was even just in a relationship. Right now I choose not to be. They're like puppies, constantly demanding attention. Needy. It hardly seems worth having to put up with in order to get a lay every now and again; less than that. In a month's time, maybe there's the potential for a few lays during one week. Sex is generally off limits during their period week, unless they're into anal. The week following they're recovering from their week of cramps, so they're bitchy. Then you have about one good week and depending on what's going on in their life or how you've pissed them off, it's hit or miss with great sex. Then the week leading up to their period, they're bitchy all over again being anxious about getting their period. And it just seems to me like an awful lot of dealing with bitchiness for minimal returns. I know it's not just about the sex, if it was, I'd stick to hookers. It's cheaper and you know you're going to get a good lay each time.

I don't see anything wrong with paying for sex. It's a business transaction; keeps the money moving in the economy and it's far more economically responsible. You have to figure going out for dinner and a show or dinner and drinks is going to cost you a hundred bucks easy. Then it's a lottery whether she's going to sleep with you, excluding the quality of lay you'll get if you do get it. You might spend all that time and money and just have her lay there missionary while you do all the work. At least with a professional you can negotiate a price and the services you'll receive. Plus you know you're getting a quality performance because their business depends on it.

I haven't used a hooker in while, but I'm not abject to the

idea. It's like the drug thing. I can't afford the risk right now. All the busts going on and then the cops plaster the poor John's faces all over the newspapers. No thanks. I've worked hard for my reputation; I don't want to throw it all away over a girl.

That's another reason, too. Get a girlfriend, what happens when you move in together? When she meets a new guy and moves out she gets half of everything you own? Fuck that. Girls are volatile as shit and this happens all the time. Guy meets girl, girl moves in, girl leaves, girl gets paid. I won't risk it. I know a guy, the most genuine and straight up guy I've ever met. I tried warning him about his girl being a total gold digging whore but he wouldn't have any of it. He loved this girl with all his heart. It made me sick. The whole time they were dating he would drive down to see her every weekend. He'd take her out, spoil her, they'd go on mini vacations. He barred no expense. He sent her flowers each week. Bought her an outrageously priced engagement ring, paid for the wedding, and then picked up his life and relocated to where her work was. He did everything. He was always the perfect guy to her. I warned him. Monogamy doesn't exist. Six months into their marriage he comes home from work early and finds her blowing another guy in their kitchen. Six months in. The sap, he tried working it out with her, wrote it off as a lapse of judgement or some other delusion. He forgave her but it didn't matter. The bitch kept doing it. When they finally split she took him to court and stole half of everything he owned. How fair is that? In my books I call that rape. Everybody makes such a big deal about 'no means no' or whatever the campaign is these days, but do you think anybody bats an eye when a girl completely fucks over a guy? The way the law is set up it's like the women have a licence to rape the shit out of men. A relationship ends and the court awards the girl the assets. In a relationship all she has to do is make one call to the police claiming domestic assault and the guy goes directly to jail. There doesn't even need to be any evidence. Guilty until proven innocent. Her word trumps all.

And then there's the go-to attention sucking line girls toss out like pennies in a well, "Oh, I was raped once." Girls throw that word around like it's going out of style. I'm so tired of hearing it. I don't even believe in rape. Every case I've ever heard of: girls fault. I mean, if a girl finds herself in a position where the possibility of rape could happen, she wanted it to happen. Case closed. Every girl tells the same story. "I was a virgin. There was this guy who was known for raping girls. We were all partying together one weekend, drinking and having a good time. I ended up sharing a bed with this guy and when I woke up in the middle of the night, we were naked and he was raping me. No I didn't report it. I couldn't handle the shame." Fuck that. You were a young girl and wanted to lose your virginity. You knew a guy who would fuck you and went to bed with him. In the morning you felt ashamed that you gave it away so easily so you called it rape. "Oh this one time, I was running through the park at night wearing short-shorts and a sports bra, when all of a sudden a guy who ran there too came out and raped me." No. A girl who doesn't want to get fucked would never put herself in the position where she could be taken by force. If it happened to her, she wanted it to happen. It's like an Ozzy Osborne concert, you go to one and you expect to see him bite the head off a bat. There was this other musician, GG Allen, he had sex with girls on stage during his shows. He'd grab a girl from the concert and just start feeding her the pipe. He said, "When a girl comes to my concert she should expect to get raped." Girls still went to his shows; and then they had the audacity to bitch about it. It's such a horrible thing to accuse someone of and we just eat the shit up. We don't even question it. She said rape, he must have done it. Even if there was no sex, but she says it, fuck him. Go directly to jail. Prove you didn't. Treacherous little bitches. Look at all those teenage girls getting teachers in trouble over false accusations; concocting stories that destroy lives all because they were feeling a little vindictive. Nobody should ever have the ability to wield that much power over someone else. Women's Lib? Equality? Not even close. Women have the power, and like anybody who has power, they keep clawing for more. It makes me sick.

That's why I'm single.

When the right girl does come along though, you can bet your bottom dollar I'll be getting my lawyer to draw up a pre-nup to protect everything I've earned. Plan the breakup while you're still friends. That's probably the only piece of advice my dad said that's worth remembering. The poor guy. My mom beat him pretty good in court. He didn't treat her very well and deserved it and all that, but fuck, he still hasn't recovered from the incident. He's living in the past and that shit will kill you. I figure, everything that's happened in the past should stay in the past. Good or bad. All the bad shit, it's over, has nothing to do with today. The good stuff, can't dwell on that either. All the good that's behind you is already part of who you are. You have to leave the past to rest; can't drive forward staring into the rear view mirror, right? Have you ever been on a boat? You know the wake it makes as it moves through the water? The wake doesn't steer where you're going.

That's a gem adage that I'm still working on.

Remember how I was telling you about my wine glass breaking and that's what provoked all this thought and me calling to come in and see you?

Well the next day I was out running some errands in town. I had to return my empties, pick up some water softener salt, and go to the bank; that sort of thing. I do everything I need to in one trip to save time and I plan the route in advance so I can drive a loop making it even more efficient. I hate waste. I left my house around one and estimated I could probably complete everything in about an hour. The first thing on my list was to return the empty wine bottles. I was driving along a back country road, the shortest route between point A and point B, and I was stuck behind a guy driving below the speed limit. I checked my blind spots to make sure nobody else was around and then signaled to pass him. When I got in front I could see hands waving angrily in my rear view mirror, but I didn't give it any thought. He was behind me so I ignored him. I'm booting along driving pretty quick, maybe going twenty kilometers over the speed limit, nothing unsafe and I forget all about the guy. When I got to the store I returned the bottles and at this location you have to return them to the drop off point behind the main store and then go inside to claim your money.

I got six bucks and change.

Coming out of the store I passed a person coming in. Because it's out in the country I greet everyone cordially but this guy responded with a glare. "It's a good afternoon for you out passing cars at 140 in a no passing zone, *uphill*," he said. I smiled, realizing this must have been the guy from way back, and said, "Excuse me?" But he wouldn't let it go. "You just think you're king shit, don't you? Do whatever the fuck you want, right?" He was a real douchebag, but I was on a timeline, so I just kept walking and said, "I don't think you know what you're talking about, sir." The guy set me right off. I should have punched him in his mouth just for confronting me in public like that. His truck was parked beside my car and I thought about keying it, but there are some things you don't do, and fucking with another man's vehicle is one of them. Instead I snapped a picture of his plates, got in my car, and drove away. Mother fucker. I couldn't shake it. The entire time I'm driving around doing what I needed, I'm thinking of this incident. It soured my whole afternoon. When I got to the bank and was standing in line at the teller, I noticed a guy with a goatee come in and start fumbling around at the ATM. I recognized him from the store where the altercation took place. It wasn't the douchebag who started the fight but it might have been one of his friends or something. Maybe they were in a gang like Hell's Angels. It could have been anything. When I left the bank, he left the bank. Before I reached my car I paused on the sidewalk to let him pass but he stayed back a few steps and paused too. I was pretty sure he was following me. I got into my car and purposely took a long time getting it started, I wanted to see if he would leave first, but he was delaying also. This confirmed my suspicion. He was definitely following me. I didn't know why he was following me, but I needed to lose him and lose him fast. When I left the parking lot I performed a bunch of evasive maneuvers to lose the tail. I've read all the survival books available, so I know how. Sure enough he was no longer behind me. Pretty much since I left the bank he was nowhere to be seen. You know what I did next? I had the licence plate of the guy from the store, so when

112

I drove home, I took a different route.

I think I might have an eidetic memory or something because I can remember pretty much everything that's ever happened to me.

I instantly recalled exactly when I first saw his vehicle before I passed him at the beginning of my errands. Where he was driving from no one would be going to the store the route he was unless he lived in the area. He couldn't have lived in town because he turned on that long stretch of road from the opposite direction so I had a pretty good idea where he originated. I drove that route home, driving the speed limit the whole time, and scanning the houses along the way. I wasn't even surprised when I approached the area where I thought he might live and saw his truck parked in a driveway. It was a house with blue siding and white trim at the end of a laneway. I drove in and parked right in front of his house, blocking the driveway. I got out and snapped another picture of his truck, this time with his house number and his wife's car in the picture. I stood there long enough for him to see me through the window before casually getting back into my car and slowly driving away. Piece of shit, approach me like that in public. By this point I didn't even care if he was connected, I had to show him I wasn't scared. He didn't know who I was; I could be a crazy person, a serial killer or something. You don't confront people with hostility, that's how people end up getting shot. He's lucky it was me he confronted and not someone else. His wife would have been really heartbroken if he confronted a murderer and wound up dead. Unless he was a piece of shit to her, too. No matter, hopefully he learned his lesson.

It's not like I'm not going to do anything to him. I just wanted to intimidate him by demonstrating how scared I wasn't. I'm just going to use the picture to look up his particulars, file it, then forget the whole thing ever happened. But if he ever calls me out in public again, or I see his buddy following me, then I'll do something. You can't let people walk all over you, or else they'll walk all over you forever, and forever is a long time.

What I did wasn't crazy. I wasn't exhibiting dangerous behaviour, and it's not paranoia either. The guy assaulted me, then had one of his friends follow me around. I can't prove he was following me, it could have been a coincidence, sure, but I doubt it. I was acting in self defense. I was protecting myself, like you do with insurance. It's not like I was stalking anybody. Do you want me to tell you the world's all sunshine and rainbows, that I had a great week, that I'm docile like everybody else? I can't do that. I'm not like everybody else and I'm fine with that. I can pretend out there but in here I have to be able to let my guard down a bit. I'm tired of pretending to be like everybody else living this secret private life that only I know about. It's exhausting. I've tried getting along by caring about the characters on TV, or the types of cars people drive, or the stats of a football team; or, fuck, talking about the weather. I've tried it all but I can't do it. None of it. Conversations are dull. For once I want someone to say, "You know what, I get why that kid shot up the school. Can you believe he only tagged fifteen kids?" That's a conversation I could get into. That's being honest. I would respect that. But no, everybody's a parrot saying, "Oh, it's such a tragedy," "That sick kid, he's so evil."

No. There has to be someone who can relate.

I can relate.

I vividly remember a time where I could have gone the

route of Eric Harris and Dylan Klebold and shot up my school. I would have taken out every single one of those spoiled little rich kids. Every jock. Every fucking *mean girl*. Lined them up and executed them one at a time. That would have been quite the experience. People aren't naturally hero's so they would just stand there crying as I picked off one after the other. Gun to forehead, "Remember when you slapped my lunch tray out of my hands?" Fuck you. Bang. Next. "Remember when you pissed on my gym clothes when I was in the shower?" Bang. Next. "Remember when you said I had a bubble butt and that all the girls thought I was gross? You're going to be quite the looker yourself with half your brain painting the wall behind you." Fuck you. Bang. Bang. Bang. Bang. Bang.

Nowadays I would do it differently. I figure I could get away with at least 60 kills. With three bullets allotted to each person, two in the chest one in the head, that's only 180 bullets. Thirty rounds to a magazine, that's six mags. You can carry at least double that so with one rifle and 12 magazines at three bullets a kid you have the potential for 120 kills. And everybody gets excited over 15? We know Eric and Dylan thought through their massacre, but I say, not as thoroughly as they should have. A little more forethought would have gone a long way.

Consider the classroom route, that's what, thirty kids in a square room with one exit? You shoot one of them and everybody else panics. I say go for the teacher first because she'll probably have her back to the class writing something on the board. Everybody freaks out and then simply start tagging all the ones closest to you. A girl peaks her head out from under the desk, shoot her. Somebody gets brave and yells at you, shoot him. Go in there expecting to get everyone and don't leave until you do. Pop. Pop. Pop. Two in the chest, one in the head. This first class execution sets the rest of the school to high alert so now everybody is locked inside their classroom; lights off, shades drawn, and students under their desks. The police have probably been called but they're not going come in the school and start shooting right away so you'll have some time. You've already got thirty kills under your belt so you just go to the next class. Build on your success. Kick in the door. Shoot the lock. Whatever. Pop. Pop. Pop. Another three magazines. Another 30 kids. That's 60 kids and you haven't even broke a sweat. Why not wait and plan your attack during an assembly? Get the whole school involved. Chain all the doors on the outside of the gym, come in through the only unlocked exit and spray everybody. Instant panic. It always is. Just keep enough distance between you and the crowd you can tag them all day. If you're going to go the assembly route you'll need more than one rifle but you could always make a few pressure cooker bombs in advance or have some pipe bombs in your backpack to start throwing. You have to be creative. The bigger the crowd means the greater number of potential casualties. Go this route and you might reach the 120 mark. I think anywhere above 60 deaths would start to impress me. When I hear on the news, 14 people died in a terrorist attack in London, I'm like, 14 people? They must have been some stupid ass terrorists. Anything you can count on your fingers and toes is pretty unremarkable.

But see. This is what I'm talking about; nobody ever has conversations remotely close to this even though I'm sure they must have thought it. Nobody has the nerve to say it out loud. Everybody lives in fear that if they something somebody else won't approve of that they'll get in trouble. That they'll be marked. That they'll lose their job.

It doesn't take any effort to be offended. It's cheap and pathetic. "Oh, I'm so offended, I'm disgusted. Look at me in all my self-righteousness." Reprimand the person who said whatever it was that offended someone else, fire them, charge them, publicly shame them, and eventually nobody says anything at all. What kind of world is that? I'm sick of it. It's the world I've been living in my entire life and I think I'm ready to flip the world off and stop worrying about what others might think. I want to live authentically, aligned with my thoughts and actions. I don't want to go out killing people and getting doped up all the time, I just want to stop pretending one thing to save face while keeping the things I think about private. I think about these things all the time. Why don't we have more school shootings? Thousands of schools operating nine months of the year and we only get one incident every couple? Then we get all jacked up about firearm regulations?

How come we don't have any powerhouse couples like Bonnie and Clyde or Paul and Karla anymore? When we do, everybody freaks out like "Oh my god, it's so terrible." There are eight billion people in the world. These types of things should be happening more often than they do. But that's not how the media portrays things. They say it getting worse and worse, but it's nothing like how it used to be.

Aren't people always mentioning the good old days? I grew up during the time while Paul Bernardo and Karla Homolka were active in the community. Even that many years ago I knew I was different. That I thought about everything differently. I was a little kid then, but I remember thinking, why not just go out take whoever you want? I didn't know

117

much about sex or about anything for that matter, but I remember thinking whoever's doing this is pretty bold. A real man's man, you know? Taking whoever the fuck he wanted. When I found out they were a girl guy team I thought that's what true love was all about. That's dedication. Monogamy might even stand a chance under those conditions.

As a little kid I would sit at the top of the stairs and listen to the news my parents watched on TV. I would hear my mom on the phone talking about the updates with her girlfriends. I was a kid. I wasn't stupid. I heard little details about the local catholic high school girls getting snatched, being found dead encased in cement or naked in a ditch. Everybody talking about it secretly, behind closed doors, "Oh the atrocity."

One day while all this was going on, my mom was driving me to baseball practice and where we lived wasn't the nicest of neighbourhoods so you'd have litter strewn about everywhere. People had cars on their front lawns and sofas on their porches. Little kids with diapers would run around with their strung out mothers calling after them. We were driving to baseball practice and in the ditch on the side of the road was a dirty, naked, life size plastic doll. Trying to impress my mom with my knowledge of current events, I pointed out the window and said, "Look mom, it's Kristen French." She was the latest girl to get snatched. Without saying a word she raised her hand and smacked my mouth so hard I saw black. The words that followed were a firehose scolding me, telling me how disgusted she was that her son could say such an awful thing. That if I ever said anything like that again she'd tell my father and he'd spank me good. We drove the rest of the way in thick tension. We never mentioned it again. I didn't ever comment how the girls from the school where they were taken from were the slutiest girls in the city, that they were known for flaunting their sexuality. That they deserved it. I never commented how I could empathize with the pair, how even at that young age I could see how someone could do that. The temptation, the rush, the power. Even then I knew I didn't belong. I knew that I was capable of extreme actions. The reality is that if I was Mr. Bernardo, if I was him down to the atomic level, I would think and behave and do exactly as he did. Period. If I was Paul Bernardo, with Paul Bernardo's genetic makeup, and Paul Bernardo's life experience, I would be Paul Bernardo and I would have done exactly what Paul Bernardo did. To think otherwise is ludicrous. If I was either Eric Harris or Dylan Klebold, I would have done precisely what Eric Harris or Dylan Klebold did. It's undeniable. It's a lie to think otherwise. There's no respectable or intelligent position to defend against this. These individuals don't know why they have homicidal inclinations any more than those who don't have murderous tendencies can explain why they don't. If they knew better they would have done better. To know and not do is not to know.

Like I said in the beginning, I can't take credit for my natural ability. I'm serious about that. I didn't choose to be born when I was, to the parents that I was born to, in the city I grew up. I had no control over my genes or my life experience. Nobody does. It's just the way I am.

I'm not condoning their actions, I know certain behaviours aren't positive contributions to civilized society; however, I'm not going to blame them either. I can't. I get it. Can I say this in public? No. Absolutely not. My tumbling, the homicidal fantasies that hijack my brain, I'm pretty sure they occur because I haven't acted on them. You know how when a guy tries to practice celibacy, no more sex, no more masturbation, all that buildup in an attempt to focus their energy somewhere else?

It's popular among the religious.

Celibacy is all good while you're awake, but as soon as you drift off to sleep your body's going to take over and force you to release the pressure. Enter wet dreams. Come everywhere. If a guy bottles up his urges long enough, the body will find a way to force his hand.

Maybe that's what my visions are like? Do you think that's why I get them, because I need to kill? I've only ever killed two things before in my entire life. One bird and one fish, both of them by accident and both of them still haunt me.

Those poor fucking creatures.

The bird I killed I shot with a pellet gun. My friend and I, a different friend than the boy I played Mission Impossible with, but at that age we're all pretty much the same. We would go out to the forest behind his house and play paintball against one another. We would explore abandoned buildings looking for treasure. We would set traps in the woods, shoot things with our pellet guns, and practice throwing knives. Every once in a while we would blow shit up. No matter who the friend was we always traversed the same activities and had the same fun.

One day we were shooting targets in the yard and became bored at how easy it was to hit stationary objects. We wanted more of a challenge and decided to shoot at the birds as they flew by. Despite his effort, my friend kept missing and was getting frustrated, so when it came my turn I didn't want to hit first try so I aimed off, leading the bird by quite a distance.

I can't believe I remember this, that's how big of an effect it had on me.

The lead I gave the bird wasn't enough and in hindsight I should have been trailing the bird, but I didn't know any better at the time. I shot him right through the chest. He fell like a rock out of the sky and made a thud as he hit the ground. It was a little bird but I felt the thud. It's the same sound anything living makes when it hits the ground: a weighty defeated thump. My friend cheered. I felt sick to my stomach. We ran over to the bird. He was dead. A tiny bit of blood soaked the feathers around where I had shot him. His wings clung formed to his sides and his little claws were tucked up tight against his chest. The fucking bird flew right into my shot. We buried him and never spoke of it again.

Killing animals did not feel good.

The fish I meant to kill, I wanted to eat it, but she didn't die the way I had planned. After I caught the fish I clubbed the top of her head to kill her and then put her limp carcass into a grocery bag to bring her home. In the kitchen I was rinsing her off in the sink when she started flapping around. I had to grab her by the tail and start beating her head against the inside of sink. Blood was squirting from her gills and spattering all over the backsplash. She kept flopping so I kept swinging her. Drops of blood were sticking to my face and on the ceiling above. That poor fish. She had a lot of fight in her. It was such a torturous experience that I lost my appetite. The only reason I ate her afterwards was because of the backstory. I felt guilty for what I'd done and not eating her would have been a waste.

You know how I feel about waste.

There're people out there who love to hunt and fish and prepare their own meats, that's not me. I can't kill animals. I wasn't born with it. People though? Maybe I'm capable. I've never had a fantasy about killing a cat or anything, it's always been people. Guys, girls, kids. It doesn't matter. I've had tumbling experiences for all of them.

Maybe I need to find an outlet to release some of this pressure, or like celibates having wet dreams I'm afraid I won't be able to control it.

I'm sure it's not going to happen anytime soon, I've been living like this for fifteen years remember, but I know it's something that should be addressed.

We're still inside the confines of confidentiality right? I really think talking with you might help me Doc. It feels good to share, to know I'm not dealing with it by myself anymore. Sometimes it's hard to see the picture when you're standing in the frame.

My relationship that ended? How much time do we have? We met online and the first time we went out, the first time I saw her in person, I walked right up and kissed her. I don't know why I did it. Well, I do, I saw it in a movie once and it worked for him so I thought I'd give it a try. She loved it. We picked up take-out and went back to her place. I always treat the first date like a litmus test; if there's no sex there's no second date. It's a quick way to determine whether you're going to be compatible with each other. Can't waste time on something you know won't pan out.

At her place, while we were eating, there was this sexual tension building. We were touching each other. We were leaning into each other. We were laughing. She started rubbing the inside of my thigh and that was it. I dropped everything and picked her up. We fucked right there in the kitchen. Against the wall; on the counter. Laying on the kitchen floor in exhaustion, we laughed, ate some more, then fucked again. I thought if this is how it was going to be, she just killed the litmus test.

The first week we were together, everywhere we ventured we had sex. In the car at the drive-in. During a walk by the river. We even did it in a change room at a Smart Set. She was fuck wild. A real nymphomaniac. Just the type of girl I need. That's not even the best part. When I reached for a condom during that first time in the kitchen, she told me not to bother. I hate condoms. I'm a real raw dog and bail kind of guy. I can't believe I hadn't met her sooner.

If I'm going to be honest with you though, the sex did get a little weird one night. She asked me to choke her. I'd never done that before so I was a little hesitant. The first time she asked me was almost a whisper, *choke me*. I pretended not to hear her but I knew exactly what she said. I have incredible hearing. A few minutes later she said it again. You know how when a guy is trying to get his dick rubbed how he'll slowly nudge your hand toward it? Leslie did the same thing except she slowly moved one of my hands up to her throat. I was uncomfortable, so I held her neck kind of loosely, very lightly like a limp hand shake. Pressing her neck into my hand she kept asking me to squeeze tighter. We're fucking, I have my hand around her throat and it's starting to turn me on, so I give her a little squeeze. Instantly I'm throbbing, she's starting to struggle so I ease off a bit. The maniac, she yelled at me, *harder*, so I gave it to her harder. I even used my second hand. Now I have two hands around her throat. She's wrangling about on the bed, trying to be free and I'm doing everything I can not to blow. In my mind I'm thinking about that bird I shot. How sick it made me feel. That worked for a bit, but this was hot. I thought about the fish I killed. I thought about whatever I could to bring me back from the edge, this whole time choking her, my adrenaline pumping, her struggling. It was fucking magic. There's no way she's not pregnant from the orgasm I blew. I couldn't wait till the next time. Usually once at night is good for me but sex like this is crack; not even an hour later we were at it again.

That was the beginning of our sexual exploits.

Choking was hot, but add restraints and it's a whole new game. She liked being tied up; hands to the head board and legs to the posts on the end of the bed. She liked being tied with her hands behind her back with her feet bound. She liked being hit. One night she bit me on the shoulder because I wouldn't hit her. I smacked her so hard she orgasmed on impact. We're fucking two or three times a night and having to drink Gatorade just to stay hydrated.

But she had to keep taking things to another level.

One night we're lying in bed after sex and I knew something was up. I knew she was feeling uncomfortable. It was the first time I'd felt that way with her. It was like she was holding something back. I'm pretty good at getting a read on people so I asked her to say whatever she needed to get off her chest. I told her I'd be fine with whatever it was. I thought she was going to tell me she had the clap or that she had a boyfriend who worked in the oil fields who was on his way home. I thought whatever it was it would be something to complicate our little fling. Either of those conclusions I could have handled; the clap's just a few pills right? And if she had a boyfriend, I'd be fine fucking whenever he wasn't around. I figured whatever she needed to say might make things difficult but whatever it was, she needed to say it. I kept pushing her until she did.

It wasn't the clap or a boyfriend.

She asked me to rape her.

After a week of ruthless fucking, a week of adding more and more violence to our sex, I didn't know what else we could possibly do. I didn't know how we could possibly spice things up even more. This was it.

Have you ever heard this type of thing before? Not like role playing either. Rape like if anybody saw it, they would believe it was a rape and call the cops.

I must sound like a pussy right now, my skepticism. It felt like we were about to cross some sort of taboo line. And then there was the semantic issue. How was I supposed to rape her if I had her consent? I didn't want to let her lay there awkwardly any longer, and logically it wasn't much different than what we'd already been doing, so I told her I would. She was brave enough to ask me, the least I could do was give it a try.

Rape brings sex to a whole new level.

The plan was that one day at my sole discretion and without warning I would take her by force. There were no limits to where it could occur or how I would do it. She wanted it as authentic as possible. I could have taken her in a parking lot, or in her house while she was sleeping, or while she was on her morning walk; anywhere my heart contended to. Her only condition was that it had to be a rape. I didn't know her, she didn't know me. I had to mask my identity, not use her name, and under no circumstance was I to stop short of a completed act. I was to use any force necessary and then disappear from the scene.

As legit as a rape can be without grabbing a stranger.

This wasn't going to be a problem. I've always been

capable of extreme actions. I already had duct tape and rope at home so I picked up a ski mask that I could wear rolled up as a beanie and bought a giant hunting knife so I could hold it against her throat as we fucked. I bought them with cash and from different stores just to be safe. Could you imagine the looks I would have got as a giant hunting knife and a black ski mask rolled down the conveyor belt toward the cashier? I'd have been a marked man by the time I pulled out my wallet to pay. I went to one of those hillbilly gun nuts at the flea market and bought a mafia blackjack. They're those lead tipped leather paddles that you see in the movies used to knock out people being kidnapped. This was the last tool I needed to complete my rape kit. I felt like a little kid all over again. Planning secret missions, gathering all the items I'd need for its success. Stalking through the forest during paintball and stalking the streets at night are pretty much the same thing. Simply a natural evolution to the games we play as kids. My whole life stalking has made me pretty stealthy on my feet. I can sneak up on just about anyone without them noticing. I hold this skill in high esteem. I remember seeing a movie when I was younger about these four bank robbers that wore rubber masks whenever they pulled a heist. The masks were painted with the faces of past presidents and for most of the movie they couldn't catch them. It wasn't until late in the movie when one of the investigators was reviewing some of the security footage from one of the bank heists that he noticed the robbers walked on the balls of their feet with their heels off the ground. They moved on the balls of their feet like a woman would while wearing heels. This observation pretty much cracked the case because in the end they discovered that the bank robbers were four women. When I saw this I immediately started walking on the balls of my feet as if I was wearing imaginary heels. You know, just in case someday I was caught on camera committing a crime I hoped an investigator would notice it and think that the suspect they were looking for was a female and serve as a red hearing in aiding my getaway. I did this as a little kid as often as I remembered to, that now it's just the way I walk. You can't believe what this did for my stealth abilities. Pretty intense, right? All my life I've been preparing for this.

So we're lying in bed when she asks me to rape her and while she's at work the next day I'm out gathering supplies. My plan was to get her that night. She wouldn't expect me to strike so quick. I wanted to grab her as she was unlocking the door when she came home from work. I felt comfortable in her house and thought it would be a good setting to use while I learned the ropes. You know, get all the kinks out before moving into the public arena. You don't just start off a star in the National Hockey League. You have to work your way up.

All day at work she was probably wondering when I'd do it, trying like a person meditating to not think about it, yet distracted the whole time. I made sure to get her when she wasn't expecting it though. You know how when you're driving home from work you can be thinking about something the entire way, something you have to do as soon as you get home, but the second you walk through the front door your mind goes blank? That's the moment I hit her.

Literally.

I snuck up behind her as she was unlocking the door and struck her in the back of her head with the blackjack. Before I'd finished the swing she crumpled into my arms so I kind of just pushed her through the open door and let her fall on the floor. I couldn't have timed it more perfectly. She was out cold.

I pulled her forward so I could shut the door behind us and then put duct tape over her mouth. I taped her wrists. Before I got started I paused to admire her lifeless body. She had skin like an angel; very pale, very smooth. She looked so helpless laying there, innocent, but I knew full well she wasn't. I tore off her pants and ripped open her blouse. Her breasts held firm in her bra as she lay there on her back. In all the excitement I almost forgot to pull down my ski mask. She would have been so pissed if she'd woke up and saw my face. You wouldn't believe how hard I was by this point. All the pre-come I was dripping would have filled a bathtub. I barely made it inside her without blowing. I pictured all the things I usually did to keep from coming, my bird and my fish; but I had to picture searing flesh and dead babies and the smell of shit just to bring me down a few notches. Anything I could think of to stop the eroticism of rape.

I swear this is going to catch on. I don't see how it can't.

Before I forced my way in, I spit on her pussy to lube her entrance. She was tight, resistant almost but the rest of her body was still limp. I started to get a little worried thinking I might have hit her too hard but after the first few thrusts she started to come around. She started struggling like a madwoman when she woke. I could hear her trying to scream. Whether she was acting or honestly scared for her life, her behaviour provoked me and I had to smack her a few times to get her to calm down. She's lucky I didn't leave any marks.

I held her by the throat to let her feel my power and she started squirming again. She had always told me to squeeze tighter, but with her mouth taped, I took the liberty to exact my own judgement. I was making sure there'd be no way for her to bitch I wasn't choking her tight enough.

The tears had her mascara running down the side of her face.

The crying convinced me the fear in her eyes were real. I think that's what was most erotic. There was nothing she could do to stop me. Even if she had gotten the tape from her mouth and begged me to stop. Even if she swore up and down that this wasn't what she wanted, I wouldn't have stopped. There was nothing she could have done to prevent me from completing the act.

Nothing.

Her eyes changed colours. Not even. Her eye's lost colour, like there should have been colour around her pupils and you could tell that once there was, but now whatever colour had been there only moments before had been brushed over with terror. Those eyes. Fuck. Even now I'm getting hard thinking about them.

When I was a little kid I thought I could understand Paul and Karla, or Harris and Klebold, I thought I could relate intellectually, but I had no fucking idea.

Rape wasn't just sex at a whole new level.

Rape was living life in a different dimension.

It is the purest form of love.

The orgasm was an eruption inside her, a God fucking Mary to birth Jesus eruption, and she knew it. I had finally become me; the person I'd longed to be my entire life. I wish I could have stayed there with her and gushed like a little girl over her first kiss, but that would have ruined everything. There were rules: I didn't know her, she didn't know me, use any force necessary, and then disappear from the scene. As far as the agreement was concerned, it wasn't even Leslie lying there. I don't know if she finished, I just got up, spit on her like the whore she pretended to be, and walked out the door leaving her there in a puddle of come, sweat, and tears.

This wasn't crossing a taboo line like I had been worried about originally. This was leaping into a world I didn't know existed.

I remember thinking she was the greatest thing that had ever happened to me.

In hindsight, I should have gone out the back door but in my haste I didn't think of it. Instead, I left the way I came and cut down the alley beside her house and through the woods to my car parked on the other side. I reached my car grinning ear to ear. Elated, I didn't think to conceal my duffle bag and tossed it in the back seat in plain sight. If by chance I would have been pulled over on my drive home, rapist grin on my face, sex juices on my pants, and the rape kit open on the back seat of my car, I would have been ripped out of the vehicle and beaten like that black guy on the side of the road, regardless whether they had a victim report. Could you imagine, "Officer, officer, I swear, she begged me to do it."

When I arrived home I was in a daze, I don't even remember the drive. I walked straight to my chair, poured a glass of wine, and drank deep the blood of Christ. I'm not religious, but at that moment I felt like God himself. I must have sat there for hours because when the phone rang and snapped me from my fog it was well after midnight. I hadn't notice it get dark outside.

On the other end of the phone was Leslie. A very, very pissed off Leslie. I'd never heard her like this before. I guess I didn't really know her all that well and knew she was bound to have a few flaws, but I was really hoping it wasn't the overreaction thing. With women though, overreaction is the only reaction, so I chuckled a bit which enraged her more. I thought she was joking but changed my tune quick when I realized she was actually angry. I couldn't believe how wide awake I still was. I couldn't believe it had taken her so long to call me, for that matter. All night I wanted to share how incredible the experience was for me. I wanted to tell her about my preparations. I wanted to ask her if she was surprised by my stealthy attack or if she had caught a glimpse of me before the strike. I wanted to find out everything but knew I'd have to wait. When a girl is freaking out, you have to let them blow off their steam or else they get all twitchy.

Her recount was epic.

Apparently one of her neighbours saw me *assault* her on the front steps and called the police. Fortunately they didn't show up until after I left, which doesn't say much for their response time or god forbid how quickly I finished. I made it last as long as I could but with all her struggling and crying I knew I blew quick. You would have too if that was your first time. Fuck was it hot.

Anyway, after I'd left, the cops showed up and were knocking on the front door, keys still dangling from the deadbolt. They saw her body lying on the floor as they looked through the window and that was enough for them to enter the house. Leslie was still bound and crying and half naked on the floor when they went in. Her makeup was smeared across her face. She said the worse part of it all was that she knew one of the officers. A friend of her dads or something.

She was beyond livid.

I thought it was hilarious but couldn't tell her. Not a chance. Not with the responding officers having to kneel over her nude body to free her hands and remove the tape from across her mouth. Not with Leslie scrambling to cover her breasts and use her pants to hide her semen soaked vagina, the whole time screaming for them to get out. No. This was not the time to point out the humor of it all. This was the time to let her vent.

The responding officers had to radio for a female officer to come to the scene, so now there's two cruisers parked outside her house. Her neighbours are standing on their porches trying to get a peek at what all the excitement was about, and I'm safe and sound sitting in my chair at home. Poor Leslie. How could she explain it? With her head still pounding from the blackjack hit, to my credit, it must have looked like a legit rape.

It was the best sex I've ever had.

As she's telling me this I'm thinking ahead as far as I can, trying to determine what her options were. We never explored the idea that someone might actually call the police over our exploit. As far as I could tell she had two options. She could tell the truth, be a little embarrassed, and blush it off. Besides, I'm sure the guys would be secretly wishing their girlfriends would let them give it a go.

That's how good rape is.

Guaranteed it's going to be the next big thing.

That was her first option I contemplated.

Her second option: she could lie. She could say she was raped. That's what the police thought it was anyway, and technically it wouldn't have been that big of a stretch. She struggled, she had marks. I don't think she expected it when it happened. If she went this route she'd have to give a statement, tell them how somebody had hit her from behind as she was coming home from work and when she woke up he was deep inside her. She could say how every time she tried to scream he slapped her, how he nearly choked her to death. They'd take pictures of her bruises. They'd collect a semen sample. Have her tested for STD's. She'd have to sit with a police sketch artist describing me with a ski mask on noting whether I had any scars or tattoos.

Leslie was an attention seeking girl and I could see her going this route to make her story all the more erotic. I'd wind up with my DNA on record and her holding it as blackmail over my head for the rest of my life. I'd have to kill the bitch and then I'd be up for rape and murder. I started getting all worked up thinking about this option. As I'm listening to her I'm thinking I should have just killed her instead of having left her there. I was silently reprimanding myself for having been so reckless. Inside I wanted to lash out but I forced myself to hear her through. She was starting to calm down and talk less wildly.

She told me how the female cop wrapped her in a blanket and had the first officers conduct their investigation outside so the two of them could be alone. Leslie's bawling. The entire time she's telling me this, I'm freaking out thinking, what the fuck did you say Leslie, what the fuck did you say? Then she started bitching at me that I hit her too hard, there's a lump on the back of her head, how she's been icing it all night. Leslie's bitching that she couldn't get her wrists free from the duct tape and that if she'd been able to then there wouldn't have ever been an incident to begin with.

Leslie's angry, because like I thought, it was the best sex she'd ever had.

My little fucking nympho.

She said next time we'd do it differently use Rohypnol or

something.

Next time.

I nearly creamed my pants hearing that shit.

Leslie told me how the whole time she's bawling she's weighing the options I'd just considered. Tell the truth or lie. How she could rationalize that it wasn't really lying to let the cops believe it was a criminal rape, I'd gotten her by surprise and all, but then she thought about my semen being on record and how that might cause me trouble down the road. If she thought of being able to blackmail me, she didn't let on. She thought about the consequence of telling them the truth, telling them how it was role play and that she never intended to cause all this excitement in the neighbourhood. She thought about the implications it would make for her at work. She thought about how regardless the decision she made, everybody in the neighbourhood would think she had been raped in her own home. People might move away in fear for their own safety. Property values would drop. She thought about how people might give her care packages to help her cope with the trauma.

She liked that last idea.

She's considering all these options and buying time while she's bawling in the arms of the female officer. She really is an exhibitionist.

I'm still freaking out trying to determine if cops are going to come crashing through my front door, but Leslie's cooling off so I know she's nearing the end of her rant.

She tells me I owe her, that I'm going to have to make it up to her, because all said and done she didn't choose either of these two options. She exercised her right not to do anything. She wouldn't give a statement. She wouldn't let them swab.

Nothing. Despite all their pleading for her to do something, all their coercion telling her it wasn't her fault, urging her give a description, despite all of this Leslie told the officers she just wanted to be left alone and asked them to leave. Bawling and apologizing was all she would give them. With nothing for the officers to do, they let her be. The neighbour who called originally gave a statement, but that was it. They had to leave.

Fucking cops, always trying to be the hero.

Goddamn neighbours too; I don't understand why people stick their noses in shit that isn't any of their business.

It wasn't their business. Peeping Tom's and Nosy Betty's. Fucking busybodies. I should go back there and teach those do-gooders a lesson to keep their mouths shut. I'm not going too, I'm just venting. It just gets me really vexed when *nobodies* are able to force the hand of organizations. What happens when teens catch on and start prank calling 9-1-1? Are they going to dispatch officers every time? It will become a game. What about organized crime? Prank call in a terrorist plot or bomb threat, maybe a crime underway in one area of the city and have officers dispatched while a real crime is being committed in a different location? I don't know. It just seems like a lot of wasted resources being spent on unreliable sources.

How often do you find out in court that an eye-witness gave testimony that was completely inaccurate? People don't even remember what they ate for dinner the night before, how can they be trusted to give precise accounts of an event they glimpsed out of the corner of their eye? I don't care how confident they are. I don't care how sincere. It's possible to be sincere and be sincerely wrong. Flat earth, right? The entire population believed the world was flat. The entire world was wrong. I know, I'm bouncing all over the place, I can't blame the police, it upsets me though that there's still good Samaritans living in our neighbourhoods. It reminds me a lot of Big Brother in 1984, everybody keeping a watchful eye. Pretty soon you're not going to be able to step out your front door without somebody calling on you for something.

No, you're right, I'm single now. I really thought it was going to work out with Leslie but she took it too far. She needed a rest after our first go at rapesex so we went back to regular choking and binding. She couldn't leave it at that, though. You know what she did? She asked me to spit in her mouth.

Of course I didn't. That's just wrong. So I ended it. Gathered my things from her place went to the liquor store and bought that Argentinean wine and well, you know the rest.

ABOUT THE AUTHOR

Andrew Lafleche is a Canadian poet, author, and journalist. Thematically, his work covers topics such as spirituality, drugs, promiscuity, and alcohol, while using a spoken style of language and blending social criticism, philosophical reflection, explicit language, and black comedy. He was born in Hamilton, Ontario and remained in the Niagara Region before enlisting with the Canadian Forces at the age of 21. Following an honourable discharge from the military in 2014, Andrew published his first book, No Diplomacy, inspired by his time serving as an infantry soldier in Afghanistan. His second book, Shameless, a collection of prose depicting depravity, was published in 2016. He is recipient of the 2016 John Newlove Poetry Award and is a contributor to various national and international publications. Connect with Andrew online at: www.AJLafleche.com.